TENOCHTITLAN

Don Sheneberger

ISBN-10:1981554777
ISBN-13:9781981554775

Time Before Time

Coatl speaks

"We come from time before time and place before place: Aztlan." The storyteller continued, "We were happy there in a place of beauty." I have heard these words all my life. I have spoken them all my life. Sometimes I wonder if they are mine or a storyteller before me from time before time. We are the Mexica. We come from Aztlan and we journey to our new home wherever that may be.

I am Coatl. I have only seen 16 suns, but I have been on this journey from Aztlan all my life. My parents before me and their parents before them. Huitzilopochtli, our god, is leading us. He told us to leave Aztlan and he watches our journey from his vantage point in the sky. Every morning we greet him as he rises over the horizon and every evening we watch him leave to battle his brothers the stars and chase his sister the moon.

Every morning I get up and do the same. For although we are on a journey to our new home these things take time. I must check the animals that travel with us. I must hunt because travelers must eat. Sometimes, as son of the priest, I get to help carry the banner of Huitzilopochtli as we travel. My father is Tenoch, the leader of the Mexica. Huitzilopochtli whispers to him directions and father speaks as the god and we follow. Father says I must listen

4

carefully during the night time for Huitzilopchtli's voice because as the son of the priest it is my responsibility to be the next priest and leader of the Mexica.

Although I am afraid of this, it is my duty and so I try to remember what I hear in the night. When I tell father my dreams he usually nods and says, "Good, listen every night. Even though you are named Coatl for Quetzalcoatl, the Serpent, Huitzilopchtli will speak to you. You will know when he speaks.

I trust my father for he has led us through difficult times. It was before I was born when my father became the high priest when he was just a few years older than me. It was during the time when Huitzilopchtli had left us with his sister Malinalxochitl. The people were not happy and father spent much time calling for Huitzilopchtli to return. After many months of prayer my father dreamt of the battles of the gods. Huitzilopchtli had heard our prayers and had returned. Huitzilopchtli put Malinalxochitl to sleep and while she was asleep we were ordered to leave where we had settled. It was a dangerous time for although Huitzilopchtli had returned as our god we were afraid of what Malinalxochitl would do. Father spent much time in prayer listening to the words of the night. Finally he was able to tell us what happened. "We come from time before time and place before place: Aztlan," he began with the traditional phrase. "We were happy there in a place of beauty, but we were treated as slaves and so left with the help of Huitzilopchtli." Although this happened before I was born I have heard the story many times so I will be able to tell it myself when I am high priest. "Huitzilopchitl put his sister to sleep and ordered us to leave and we left following Huitzilopchitl. When Malinalxochitl woke she realized that she was alone and became furious that she had been deceived by her brother and determined to take revenge." Here is where we children would shiver with excitement as the thought of the gods fighting over us. "Malinalxochitl became pregnant and gave birth to Copil and Copil came in search for Huitzilopchitl and us his followers." Here the children and adults would cry out as our future lay in the balance. "Huitzilopchitli killed Copil and cut out his heart and threw it across the sky." Here we would all breathe a sigh of relief as we knew that we were now safe under the care of Huitzilopchitl.

And so we followed my father throughout the years of my childhood as he listened to the whispers of Huitzilopchitl. We knew that we must continue traveling south from our home in Atzlan that nobody alive knew. We knew we were safe because each morning Huitzilopchitl returned from his journey through the underworld where he fought his brothers to emerge victorious.

Although the people were happy under the leadership of my father I sensed worry that we did not know where we were going. My father sensed it too and prayed that Huitzilopchitl would tell him what to do or how we would know that we had found a new home. This went on for several months as father struggled to listen to the voice of the god. Finally one night he began the story, "We come from time before time and place before place,' I listened to the familiar words comfortable in the security of the story. "In those days we were known as Azteca but Huitzilopchitl led us out of Atzlan and said 'You shall no longer be known as Azteca. You shall call yourself Mexica' and so we continued on our journey as Mexica. We are the Mexica. We come from Aztlan and we journey to our new home wherever that may be." We knew the story well, but tonight father added something that would change our lives. "We are Mexica in search of our homeland and Huitzilopchitl tells us that this shall be the sign that we have found our home. 'When you see an eagle sitting on a cactus eating a snake you will know that you have found your home.'"

I had grown so accustomed to the story that the new words were a shock. Around me I saw the shock on the faces of the Mexica. We had new words from the god and his voice Tenoch, my father. Although it was late and we usually went to bed after the story time of the evening everybody was excited and the banner of Huitzilopchitl was carried around the camp to the cheers of the followers.

The next day as we continued our journey the children running ahead of the tribe shouted that they would be the first to see an eagle eating a snake. Father laughed as the children ran back and forth in excitement. "I think they have scared any eagles far away and the snakes for sure have hidden."

One day became another as we continued our journey. Now we had something to search for although we knew not where or when we would find our homeland. I also continued to listen for Huitzilopchitl at night. Sometimes I thought I heard him and sometimes I was sure it was just the wind. Father told me to keep listening and I would know when it was right.

Our journey south was not always pleasant. Although we were a small group we were large enough to worry other tribes on our way south. Sometimes they let us pass when we assured them that we were on our way south to where Huitzilopchitl was leading us. Sometimes we had to fight, but we fought under the banner of Huitzilopchitl. We knew that he fought his brothers each night with the help of the souls of fallen soldiers. These soldiers would return as the hummingbirds that we saw so frequently with the light of Huitzilopchitl reflecting off their wings. Huitzilopchitl was Hummingbird South and depicted on the banner that went before us.

That day started out as any other day. My father asked me if I had heard Huitzilopchitl in the night. I told him my dreams and as usual he said "Don't worry. He will speak to you. You will know when he speaks." We continued on with the banner of Huitzilopchitl leading us and we came to an empty village. Sometimes in our travels we came to empty villages because the people were afraid and fled in to the surrounding woods to hide from us. In those cases we went through because we had no fight with them but only wished to continue south in our search for a homeland. Today was to be different. As we passed through the empty village my father heard the rustle of feet and ordered the soldiers to the front of the tribe. He himself took the lead as the women and children stayed behind. I was proud to finally be considered a man and join the first row of soldiers as we picked our way through the empty village. The rustle of feet that my father had heard no louder than the brush of hummingbird wings was the sound of soldiers preparing for battle. With a cry they were upon us and we fought hand to hand with knives of sharpened stone. It was an equal fight with both sides numbering about 100 soldiers. I shouted to Huitzilopchitl to protect me and I heard my father shouting encouragement to the soldiers. I saw some of our soldiers drop from wounds, but I saw more of their soldiers die as we advanced and crushed their bodies under our feet. Finally the other soldiers realized that they would lose and started to retreat in to the woods. Our soldiers, sensing victory, let out a cheer and started to gather around my father. It was at that moment that one of the "dead" soldiers jumped up from where he lay and attacked my father with a stone knife shouting something in his language. Although our soldiers subdued him immediately it was too late for my father. He was on the ground with blood pouring from a wound to his side. The soldiers pulled me forward to my father's side and I heard him whisper "Don't worry. He will speak to you. You will know when he speaks." With that he closed his eyes and died.

I sat there on the ground next to his body silently asking Huitzilopchitl to make this be a dream. That I would wake up to my father's laugh and my mother's breakfast. It was not to be. I was now the leader of the Mexica. The soldiers asked me what to do with my father's body. In my first command as leader of the Mexica I said that we would stand vigil with my father as he spent his first night fighting with Huitzilopchitl against his brothers. Then the soldiers asked me about the man who had killed my father. He had been captured and not killed. I ordered that he be guarded for the night and I would ask of Huitzilopchitl what to do.

We passed the night with some soldiers surrounding my father and I in prayer asking the god what to do. In the morning I gathered the Mexica together "We come from time before time and place before place: Aztlan. Today we mourn our leader Tenoch who now fights with Huitzilopchitl. Huitzilopchitl calls for blood sacrifice to help him in his nightly battle against his brothers. If he does not receive his sacrifice he is danger of becoming weak and we Mexica are in danger of our lives." I had them bring forward the soldier who had killed my father and continued, "Huitzilcopchitl commands that from this day forward on this day of Toxcatl we shall sacrifice to him to give him power to fight each night and power to continue the 52 year calendar." With that I had the soldiers throw the captive to the ground and pull off his clothing. The man, sensing his fate, started to struggle but was soon naked as I stood over him knife in hand. With fury in my arms and the strength of Huitzilohchitl in my heart I drove the knife into his chest and ripped out his beating heart. I shouted, "We come from time before time and place before place. We are Mexica!"

The soldiers felt my blood lust and dove in on the now dead captive to cut arm from body and head from neck. Soon the body had been thrown into the fire and I was left holding the heart. I let the blood pour over my head as I reveled in the victory and revenge for my father's death. Huitzilochitl would have his sacrifice and I would be the leader of the Mexica. I saw a glint of hummingbird wing and I knew my father was happy.

The next day we continued our journey with me now leading instead of walking by my father's side. The forest seemed empty, as though the villagers knew what had happened and fled even deeper in the forest. I vowed that we would never be taken by surprise again and sent runners ahead to scout our path. In the distance to the south I saw mountains and when a hummingbird darted in front of me I took that as a sign from the god. "Forward." I said. "We are heading to the mountains."

The journey to the mountains took several months as we climbed mountains only to find more mountains beyond. I began to doubt my leadership, but I still felt Huitzilopchitl leading me as he had the night of my father's death. Finally we began to descend into a valley surrounded by the mountains, the tallest of which was smoking. We set camp for the night and as the sun set I could see light reflecting off the water of a lake. I determined that the next morning I and several soldiers would explore the lake.

Waking early the next morning I called for several of my soldiers and young men to follow me on to explore the lake. We left some of the older soldiers in charge of the still sleeping camp and made our way through the dawn. As we approached the lake we saw an island and on the island in clear sight of all was an eagle sitting on a cactus eating a serpent. Our journey was over. "We come from time before time and place before place. We are Mexica and this is our home. It shall be called Tenochtitlan."

Tenochtitlan

Cuauhtemoc Speaks

There is change here in Tenochtitlan. I can sense it even without reports of strange buildings at sea off the coast. Runners from the coast bring news of white men in large canoes stopping at various places along the coast. We know that there are white men near the coast. My runners tell me that some have been captured and offered as sacrifice to Huitzilopochtli. At least one escaped, but no matter, he will be caught again and his body will become food for the priests.

Our city is great because Huitzilopochtli has guided us since before time began. He is our war god, and as such, demands blood sacrifices. He must be kept strong for his nightly battle in the underworld. If he is not nourished with the blood of captives or slaves he could lose his nightly battle and we would cease to exist.

Our island home of markets, gardens, and of course altars must survive. This island nation lives in the shadow of the smoking mountains. Our various islands are connected by bridges to each other and the mainland. In case of attack we can easily raise the bridges to keep our people safe while our soldiers in canoes can repel any enemy. We bring fresh water from Chapultepec at the far end of the lake while night waste is taken by canoe to the other side of the lake. Our altars and temples rise above the city where the priests offer sacrifice. The captive is taken to the highest tower of the temple and from there stretched across the sacrificial stone where the priests cut open his chest to pull his still beating heart from his body and given as sacrifice to Huitzilopochtli. The body is then thrown down the steps to be consumed by the priests. All soldiers are responsible to capture slaves or enemy soldiers for sacrifice. I, of course, have captured many enemies for sacrifice.

When I was young I didn't understand why a sacrifice was necessary, but my father explained it to me. "The gods must be kept nourished just like you and I are. You get hungry each morning and afternoon don't you?" When I replied "Yes," he said, "And you get cross with your mother or sisters if you don't get food, don't you?" I smiled shyly at that, because he knew that to be true. I had thrown a tantrum that morning because I was hungry. Mother gave me a big breakfast and I felt much better and helped her with the chores. "So you see," said my father, "Just like you need nourishment to keep you strong we give nourishment to Huitzilopochtli to keep him happy. This has been done since the days of the great prophet Tenoch and time before time." I thought then and asked, "What about the people who go to Huitzilopochtli on the stone? Are they happy?" My father smiled at my concern. "Of course they are happy. They know that they are nourishing the god and will be with him forever. Yes, they might look afraid right before they meet Huitziloopochtli at the stone, but that is only momentary and soon they are with him."

Our Tlatoani, my cousin, Montezuma is responsible for the safety and security of the empire. He too, has captured enemies for sacrifice and as Tlatoani has sacrificed captives to the god. He will know of the rumors from the sea. I will ask him what it portends. Montezuma, our Tlatoani, is our elected leader by the noblemen. He leads us in battle. He confers with the priests and listens to the god. But for now I will sleep.

The next day I went across the lake to the home of Montezuma. He is godhead so I dare not look on his face. Today he is wearing ceremonial robes of feathers and special loincloth embroidered with gold and jewels. "My cousin! What brings you here today?" he asked. "My great Tlatoani I hear rumors from my runners that there are houses at sea bringing white men to our shores." I asked. "Yes my cousin. That is true. They have stopped at various villages along the coast. I have ordered my runners to report to me where they are and what they are doing." I questioned the other rumor that I had heard, "Oh great Tlatoani. I hear talk among my soldiers that this house at sea might be Quetzalcoatl returning from the East. They say that the signs are there. He is arriving in a large house. He is white with a black beard. Next year is a One Reed Year which they say will be a year of his return." Montezuma looked at me wearily. "Yes. I know the stories too. I have sent a captive with some of the emissaries. If this man is Quetzalcoatl he might want to receive a sacrifice. We will watch and look for the omens. I will personally sacrifice captives to Huitzilopochtli to ask his help."

I returned to the other side of the lake not feeling any better than I had this morning. I don't think these arrivals are Quetzalcoatl returning. There have been white men on our shore before. My runners tell me of a house at sea like what is out there now that crashed ashore. Most were killed but the rest were taken as prisoners and sacrificed except for the one or two who escaped. They were not treated as Quetzalcoatl. Quetzalcoatl is the brother of Huitzilopochtli but he is not a god of war and does not require the blood of captives for nourishment. They say he does not require sacrifice. By this time I had returned to my house across the lake and sat in my chair by the water. My servants brought me some chocolate to drink, but I was so lost in thought I didn't notice.

Cuba

Esteban speaks

I am a long way from Spain in Cuba and nearly ready
to go further in search of gold. I am Esteban Velazquez, a
some time sailor, investor, adventurer, and if you listen to
my father a full time gad about. That is why I landed here
in Cuba on the other end of the known world. My father in
Spain believes, maybe with reason, that I need to grow up
and be a man. He believes that I need to learn how to
manage business and our interests in Cuba. I am not
opposed to learning business and the ins and outs of our
interests here in Cuba. I am more interested in adventure.
My father felt that I was at the point of embarrassing our
name in Spain and so sent me here. I suppose if I
embarrassed his name here it wouldn't be as bad as
making a fool of myself in front of the king. Here in Cuba
in the year of our Lord 1518 Spain is making settlements
and plantations in Cuba. It has not been that long since
Cristobal Colon made his voyage to the Indies and there
are rumors that there are more lands or islands to the west.
Lands filled with silver and gold. Gold! That was the word
that excited me! If I could be part of a journey of
exploration and claim gold I would be rich. I could return
to Spain a rich man worthy of my father's pride.

17

As I said Cristobol Colon made his first voyage of discovery in 1492 and has been in our minds since then. He died when I was four years old, but my father remembers the stories about his explorations. Colon was sure that he had found another route to China. Now of course we think that the earth is really much larger than Colon thought and there is a new world between Europe and China. When I was young my friend Juan and I would play explorer. I was Colon and Juan another captain of his three ships. We would explore throughout Segovia and "claim" various findings in the name of the king. In the end we would always bring home our "discoveries" home to my mother who would have to serve as the Queen since we were not yet allowed before the court. Mother never knew that our discoveries of bread or fruit were stolen from the shop owners of Segovia. Juan and I were happy in our explorations and I am sure that this started my longing for adventure.

"Esteban, are you listening?" My uncle questioned. "Yes Sir!" I lied. My mind had wondered off at the thought of gold. "If I can get Cortez to lead a voyage of discovery to the West I will place you on board as my eyes and ears. We shall have to be careful. It is known that you are my nephew but we must put on a show that you are estranged from me. I want you to be my eyes and ears, but I also want Cortez to trust you as a member of his staff."

My thoughts wondered again. I thought back through my life and how I got here. I don't think I've been especially irresponsible, but perhaps adventurous. "High spirited," said my mother on more than one occasion. When I was a boy in the Segovia region of Spain I liked to dare my friends and play jokes on anybody. Now you have to remember that my father is wealthy with farm lands and textile mills. He, of course, is loyal to the king and the king has granted him estates and power at court. He would like me to follow in his footsteps as a powerful land owner and member of court. These tricks and jokes, although funny with my friends did not make him happy. One time several years ago when I was but fourteen or fifteen years old I was with some friends, "See the arches there?" Juan questioned. "See the arches!" I laughed back. They've only been there 1000 years. Of course I see them." Juan meant the aqueduct that brings water to the town from the mountains. "I bet you that nobody pays attention to them anymore," said Juan, "everybody is so intent on their own lives down here that they don't pay attention to anything else. Why I bet you we could run atop the arches and nobody would notice." I wasn't about to let that dare go unchallenged. "I think you would be afraid. I don't think you'll do it." I challenged. The arches are pretty high at least 80-100 hands tall at the highest so people below might not see what's above. "OK. I'll run, but if I run you have to run too. Naked." Of course I wasn't going to back down on a challenge. We went outside the city where the aqueduct began in the mountains at a spring. Juan said, "I'll run first and then you follow. I'll take your clothes now so you have to follow me." He concluded with a smile. "I'll wait at the other end with your clothes." So I stripped down and handed my clothes to him. He took off running across the aqueduct and he was right. Nobody paid attention to him. Women on the way to the market were talking with others. Market owners were busy taking care of their wares. Nobody paid attention to a fifteen year old running across the aqueduct. Juan made it across the aqueduct to town and waved at me. Nobody had seen him. It was a long way across the aqueduct but I could see him waving my trousers in one hand and shirt in another. I took off as fast as I could anxious to show that I didn't back down on a dare. When I was a little more than halfway across I saw that nobody was paying attention on the ground and Juan was still waving my trousers. I got a little closer to Juan and saw him jump down from the top of the aqueduct and start down the building the aqueduct abutted. "Look!" He shouted, pointing in my direction. "Somebody is running across the aqueduct!" There I was, naked in view of all Segovia. By now people did notice and started pointing. Juan had made it all the way to the ground and had joined the throng pointing at me. My clothes lie in a pile at his feet. I felt embarrassment and tried to cover my manhood with my hands but was unbalanced on the narrow aqueduct and had to raise my arms out to my sides to give me balance. I made it the rest of the way across the aqueduct to town and started climbing down to the catcalls of friends and laughter of the men of the market, the women having conveniently moved on to the church. I had to admit that Juan had dared me and I had fallen totally for it. I wasn't mad at Juan. In fact he earned my respect for beating me at the dare. I got to the ground, "You got me!" I laughed as I started to reach for my clothes, "I'll get back at you though." With my trousers in one hand I started to shake Juan's hand to congratulate him when we heard, "If you have this much free time on your hands I think we can find something else for you to do." My father was standing behind Juan with the parish priest Fr. Alonzo. "Yes boys. I think we can find something constructive to do," said the priest.

So that is how Juan and I found ourselves polishing silver in the sacristy of the church. "You should have seen your face when I yelled," Juan laughed as he picked up another chalice. "You grabbed yourself, but then couldn't walk without balancing yourself. You were doing that the rest of the way across the aqueduct." I laughed. I wasn't mad at my friend. We could never stay upset at each other. We had too much fun. "Hey. Here is the sacramental wine. Let's have a drink." I said. We opened the bottle and poured ourselves a big glass of the wine and then we had another. After several drinks we were feeling happy and I saw the statue of the Virgin in the corner. It was the statue that was used in procession. "There's the Virgin. Let's have some fun and put Fr. Alonzo's hat on her." The statue was covered ready for a procession the next day. We uncovered her, and finding Fr. Alonzo's hat we put it on her head and covered her up again. "Tomorrow when the procession starts they will uncover her and see the hat. It will be great." I said. Juan laughed as we finished our work and went home.

As we left the sacristy I saw the alms jar where people left money for candles or to give to the poor. "Look! There's enough money there for us to buy beer." Juan looked taken aback. "We can't steal from the church. It's stealing from God." "No" I replied. It's for the poor and we are pretty poor. Besides. We won't take all the money. Just enough to buy what we need." And so began my lust for gold and money. I loved the feel of coins in my pocket knowing that I could buy what I wanted. Even though I was only about fifteen at the time I made a vow that I would never be poor. I would do what I had to do to have the money I craved.

I chuckled to myself in my uncle's office as I remembered these events. The procession started and the people leading the procession pulled off the covering to see Fr. Alonzo's hat on the Virgin. It didn't take too long to figure out who was responsible and we each received a beating. It didn't quench our thirst for adventure or our friendship. Fr. Alonzo didn't allow us to work in the sacristy anymore.

Although we didn't work in the sacristy anymore he didn't notice the alms jar had less money in it each week than usual. Our parents also never noticed that Juan and I always had a few coins in our pockets and a ready wad of tobacco.

The following year I must have been sixteen Juan and I developed an interest in women. Of course that much is normal. There are always girls willing to sell themselves to willing young men. That has been a part of life since time began. With the money we collected from the alms plate we had enough to pay for our pleasure, sometimes on the street and sometimes with a willing local girl. One time I was going after a girl who seemed like she would make a good conquest. I saw her on the Sunday afternoon walkabout when young men would walk around the city center in one large circle while the young women would walk in a circle the opposite direction. In the moments that the music stopped the circles stopped moving and the couples had a chance to talk to each other under close supervision. Sylvia was a beautiful girl and I was sure that I could conquer and couple with her. During the music and circling time I slowed down whenever I got close to Sylvia and sped up once we passed. I'm sure the other boys, or should I say young men, were upset at me, but I didn't care. The music finally stopped and I was in front of Sylvia. I leaned in as close as I dared and whispered. "I'll be outside your window this evening an hour after sunset. Open it for me and I'll climb up." Sylvia blushed but whispered "yes." I left the square ecstatic knowing that that evening I would add another girl to my list of conquests. An hour after sunset I walked the short distance to her house and saw an open window at the side of the house. I quietly went to the side of the house and saw it would be fairly easy to climb using the space between the building stones as handholds and toeholds. I made it to the second level of the house and pulled myself through the window with a smile at Sylvia sitting inside at a small dressing table. She was wearing a heavy robe to ward off the fall air, but I imagined pulling the robe off and guiding her to the bed. She looked at me with an inviting smile. "You came." I started toward her, but she stopped me with a motion, "No. Stay right there I want to look at you." I was getting excited just being in the same room with her and I felt some stirrings in my trousers. "Now take off your shirt." She commanded. I willingly pulled it off and stood there waiting for her to invite me closer. "Now take off your trousers and let me see how big you are." By that time my cock was bursting at the fabric of my trousers and by the time I dropped my trousers and stepped out of them I felt that my cock was ready to explode. I started to take a step toward Sylvia when an explosion from the closet stopped me in my steps. "What do you think you're doing?" shouted one of two men who jumped out of the closet. I realized too late that I had been seen out from the start. Sylvia had obviously told her brothers and had them wait for me in the closet. I was grabbed by the arms and held tight while one brother kicked me in the balls and the other whispered . "You're going to stay away from our sister or worse will happen." I lay on the floor clutching my balls and rapidly shriveling cock while another kick penetrated my arms and landed full on my chest. "Do you understand?" came the question from the larger brother while he aimed a kick at my ass. I moaned as I was pulled to my feet. "You didn't answer me." And another kick that missed my cock, but landed full on my stomach. I doubled over in pain but was quickly pulled up straight again as the largest brother took my balls in his hand and twisted till I was doubled over in pain. "Are you coming here again?" he questioned, twisting my balls tightly in his hand while I cried and tried to double over. "No." I finally whispered and my balls were released. "Good. Now you're leaving the same way you came in," and I was pulled to the window and dropped by my arms to the soft ground underneath. "And don't even think about coming back for your clothes." I lay on the ground moaning for awhile and finally got up to walk back home grateful that it was a moonless night and I wouldn't be seen by the whole city.

The next Sunday I attempted the great circle walk again and unfortunately the first girl I stopped at was Sylvia. She smiled and said "You must come calling on me sometime." I finally admitted to Juan what had happened and he howled with laughter.

That wasn't enough for us. We wanted a challenge and we wouldn't stop till we had succeeded. We set our sights on the wife of the mayor. She was a beautiful woman, and being married, totally out of our sights. This made the challenge all the better. We schemed how we would meet her and convince her that one of us was for her. The one who succeeded in coupling with her was the winner of the challenge. We planned it carefully to be introduced to her at a party with her husband at her side. From there we would work to beat the challenge. We were presented to Maria at an afternoon garden party for the city. We each bowed and made our greetings and I talked to her first while Juan made small talk with her husband. Later we switched and Juan talked with her while I chatted with the mayor. I think we made an impression for a few days later I was called to deliver some papers to the mayor's house. To my surprise Juan arrived at the door nearly the same time. "Damn," he said, "I thought that I was the only one called and I would win." Maria herself answered the door and thanked us for delivering the papers, "But surely you are thirsty," she said. "Come upstairs where I have some wine." We both went upstairs, glancing at each other for our good luck, but also wondering why we were both here. "I'm so glad you both came for I have thought about both of you." She said, running her hands through our hair. I glanced over at Juan. We had wanted this, but didn't think it would be the two of us together. "My husband is a busy man and never at home," she began. "I'm often lonely and need companionship." She said loosening my shirt and then tugging at Juan's jacket. I looked over at Juan and saw the fear in my eyes reflected in his. I might have been afraid, but I also wanted to complete the challenge. Soon Juan and I were naked in front of the fully clothed Maria while she stroked us into firmness. This was not how I had envisioned it. Suddenly there was a sound as the front door below opened and closed. "Quick! It's my husband. You must leave." Picking up our clothes from the bed she threw them out the window. "Leave now!" She said as she left the bedroom and locked it behind her. Our only exit was naked through the window. "It looks like I finally got you back for the aqueduct" I said, trying to cover my rapidly shrinking cock. "I think I should win." He replied. "See. I'm still hard and you have nothing. Let's go before we're seen."

We had managed to escape the mayor's house and find our clothes, but I don't know if we escaped notice. The following week I was called before my father. "You have been creating rumors about town and I'm afraid you will disgrace the family name. I will not allow that or my position at court to be diminished." I stood, slightly embarrassed and somewhat sorry for my actions. He said nothing about Maria or Sylvia, but I had certainly done enough without them to cause problems. "Yes sir. I'm sorry. I'll try to do better." Not expecting what I would hear next. "It's too late for sorry. It's time you had a different education. Your uncle is now officially the governor of Cuba. I'm sending you there to manage our lands. You will be far away from the city and the estate managers will keep you busy. I expect monthly reports and your cock shriveled."

I was taken aback by my sudden change in fortunes. True, I had shown some "high spirits" around the city, but I never thought that I would be sent to Cuba, away from friends and easy access to my father's money. I vowed that I would make money in the new world. If not to make my father proud, at least to make me wealthy.

I heard my uncle say something about finances and royal assents. I paid no attention. My mind was on gold. It hadn't taken my father long to arrange passage on a ship to Cuba. Cristobol Colon had made the famous voyage searching for India less than 40 years previous. The new world was largely undiscovered, but Cuba had plantations aplenty and I was to be the latest victim, sent willingly or unwillingly to learn responsibility. The rich landowners of Spain had been granted land to develop in Cuba. Some landowners depended on local help to manage the property as my father had done. Other landowners came themselves out of a sense of adventure or failing finances at home. Other landowners, such as my father, found a new use for difficult children. "I expect you to learn management skills so that someday you can come back to your place here in Spain" were the last words my father said as we parted at the ship. I spent my seventeenth birthday on board a ship for Cuba.

Onboard I discovered a new world of the sailors and the sea. My father had paid for my voyage but I was not going first class. I bunked with several other men my age who were also being sent to the new world. Since we were all seventeen or eighteen years old and on our way to a new adventure we were all, as my mother said, "high spirited." Some of the sailors were our age, sent to sea by misfortune or adventure, and we gathered as often as their duties allowed to play cards or drink smuggled rum. "There's gold everywhere in the new world," said one of the crew on the ship. "They say that ships come back to Cuba with gold and even the sailors are rich." Another sailor said, "And why aren't you rich then? You talk big with no action. Besides. Haven't you heard about the ships that went out and never came back." The first sailor laughed, "Maybe I will become rich. I'll sign myself up for one of the voyages of discovery. It's about as safe as anything we do on the sea." I probably didn't hear the second sailor. I knew that gold would not be easy to get, but that's the challenge. Challenge and adventure. I smiled, "High spirits." As the two sailors looked at me with amusement. I knew that I had found my next challenge. This time I wouldn't have my father stopping me. I would find a way to the new world.

The voyage was uneventful in fact, but I learned about shipboard discipline. Since us young men had a natural affinity with the young sailors we spent time playing cards or general horseplay to the consternation of the ship's officers. One day when we had been at horseplay another young man named Gabriel on the ship from Madrid and I decided to have some fun with another one of our group. "Hey Alejandro," I said to the the sailor who played cards with us and supplied us with rum sometimes. "Let's play a trick on Leonardo." Leonardo was another young man from Segovia who also had been sent by his father to Cuba. Leonardo was like me, in that he was always seeking adventure, and with a ready smile and hearty laugh he could take a joke as well as give one. Unlike me, he seemed to realize this was his last chance to grow up and was taking seriously his new position. "Leonardo won last night at cards and boasted that he would take us again tonight. Let's grab his money now and then tonight when he wants to play he will have nothing." Alejandro thought that was a great idea, "He always keeps his money in a bag around his neck. I can cut the cord without him noticing and get the bag easily. I'll throw it to you." I continued, "and then tonight when we play cards he will reach for his money and there will be none. Then we can tell him. He'll think it's funny after he gets over the shock." We planed the 'heist' for later as we headed to eat. Gabriel was in the lead and pretended to stoop down right in front of Leonardo while Alejandro was walking behind. Leonardo tripped over Gabriel and in the confusion while Alejandro and I attempted to help him up Alejandro cut the cord and grabbed the bag and started to hand it off to me. Leonardo suspected nothing and I could already see in my mind the shock on Leonardo's face that evening when he discovered that he had no money to play cards. "Stop right there," came a commanding voice. We looked up to see one of the officers who had turned the corner just in time to see the

bag of money being cut from Leonardo's neck.
Alejandro's face turned white as he stood with the bag still
in his hand. Too late he let it fall to the deck. "You
sailors!" He shouted at two sailors standing nearby. "Take
this man to the brig," and then to another officer nearby,
"Inform the captain that we have caught a thief." I jumped
in and tried to talk to the officer. "Sir. It was a joke.
Gabriel and I are trying to play a joke on Leonardo.
Leonardo won our money last night at cards. We were…"
and the captain, who had by now walked up behind his
officer concluded. "You were trying to steal it back. You
three to your cabin and you shall learn about shipboard
discipline later." We were escorted to our cabin by another
young crew member who had also lost last night at cards.
"Joaquin, what will happen? You know it was a joke." I
asked whispering with the cabin door slightly ajar so we
couldn't be seen. Joaquin, standing guard whispered out of
the side of his mouth to avoid being seen. "I don't know. I
don't think the captain believes you. Theft onboard ship is
punishable by flogging." My stomach fell when I heard
that. I didn't think that something like that would ever
happen. "You mean Gabriel and I will be flogged over a
joke?" I questioned. "Not you, idiot. Alejandro. He's the
one who was caught with the money. Now get back in
your cabin. I don't want to get in trouble by talking to you
now." We were shut up in the cabin and Gabriel and I tried
to tell Leonardo what had happened, "It was supposed to
be a joke," Gabriele said, "We wanted to see your face

when you realized you had no money for cards." Leonardo looked serious, "I'm sorry. I wish that I had never played cards last night." "It's not your fault." I said. "I asked Alejandro to help us." The three of us settled in glum silence as we waited to see what would happen. A couple hours later we were called to the captain's cabin. "You three have caused problems since you came aboard this ship." I saw Leonardo's face fall. As easily the most mature of the three he was the most affected by criticism. "Please sir, We just were playing cards and they wanted to play a joke on me. I would have thought it funny. Don't punish Alejandro for our jokes." I added, "Yes sir. It was just a joke between the three of us. We should be punished." The captain looked serious. "You think this is all one big lark don't you? You came aboard thinking you could carry on the party life you have lived. This is shipboard life and we must have discipline. You shall learn about shipboard discipline. Unfortunately I can't punish you as I would like since you are passengers and not crew. I can require your presence at shipboard punishment. Tomorrow at 6 bells the seaman will be punished in accordance with naval law. You will be stationed in the front row to observe and hopefully learn shipboard discipline." Then looking at the young sailor who had brought us to the captain he concluded. "Now you young sailors who seemed to enjoy spending so much time playing cards and forgetting your duty will guard these men who will remain in their cabin for the rest of the voyage. You will do this on your own time after your shifts are finished. You will not carry on conversations or play midnight card games. Is that understood?" The sailor, whose name was David, responded with a perfect, "Yes sir." The captain glanced at the three of us and said, "Take them to the cabin and tomorrow at 6 bells make sure they are in the front row for general quarters and punishment."

David escorted us back to the cabin and we sat there in silence. I tried to whisper out the door as I had earlier, "David, what is punishment under naval law?" David was having none of it and whispered back harshly, "Didn't you hear the captain? I can't talk to you anymore." And then with a final whisper, "naval law says flogging. Two dozen lashes." We sat on our bunks in silence. Leonardo was in near tears, "We were just having fun playing cards and biding the time while we sailed to Cuba. We didn't mean to hurt anybody." Gabriel interrupted. "It's not your fault. Esteban and I just wanted to play a joke on you for winning all our money last night. I could have been the one to take your purse, but Alejandro was there while we were talking." I tried to shoulder blame,"Yes. He just happened to be there and I asked if he wanted to play a joke on you. It wasn't his fault and it wasn't your fault." We passed a quiet evening since we weren't allowed to leave the cabin. A cold meal was brought to us sometime in the evening after sunset and a slop bucket was placed on the floor. "Captain says you're not allowed to leave the cabin for the remainder of the voyage. Here's a slop bucket. Don't spill."

We passed a sleepless night with little talk. The next morning at sunrise bread and water were brought to the cabin and the slop bucket emptied. Our nerves brought us to the bucket throughout the morning with little results to show for it. "I wish we could just get it over with," Leonardo said. "I can't stand the waiting." I agreed, "Maybe the captain would punish me instead of Alejandro. I'll ask. I started it all." Lunchtime came with more bread and a little watery soup and more nervous trips to the bucket. Finally in mid afternoon 6 bells sounded with the announcement, "All hands to general quarters to witness punishment." We were brought to the main deck where we were placed to one side of the deck with the rest of the crew behind or on the other side of the deck. Soon a shirtless Alejandro was brought to the wall below the quarter deck and made to look up at the captain who stood above. "You have been caught stealing and according to naval law I sentence you to be flogged. Bosun, two dozen lashes." Before he could finish the sentence I blurted out, "No sir. Punish me. It was just a joke." I couldn't finish the words as I was punched by another sailor. "Quiet while the captain pronounces sentence." I ignored him and tried again. "Sir," this time a harder punch and the captain glared at me. "Bind and gag him. He must not interfere in ship discipline. All proceedings were stopped while I was bound and gagged by the crew. "You can't interfere," whispered David as he placed the gag in my mouth. "Don't you understand. We all knew the rules when we came aboard. It's ship life. Don't interfere." Once I was bound and gagged and made to stand Alejandro was brought forward again. His arms were raised above his head and stretched spread eagle till his feet barely touched the deck. His hands were fastened to the railing above while his legs tied to bolts mounted in the wall below. Once secure the captain announced, "Hats off. Mister. Do your duty." All the sailors removed their hats and the air was broken by the sound of the lash and a scream from Alejandro. This continued for two dozen lashes as Alejandro screamed out through the silence of the crew and I shook with muffled cries and tears running down my face as I faced my first real meeting with justice.

The punishment over, Alejandro was cut down and fell to the deck with his back bleeding. A bucket of sea water was thrown over the wounds to clean them which brought more screams from Alejandro and more crying from me. The captain looked at us. Gabriel and Leonardo were white with fear and were trembling. I was crying with tears going down my cheeks and soaking the gag that had been placed in my mouth. Spittle was working its way through the gag and I could barely breathe. The captain looked at us, "Send them back to their cabin. They are not to move from their bunks the rest of the day." Then, looking at me, "Keep him bound and gagged till dog watch. Maybe he will learn not to interrupt ship discipline." We were brought back in silence to our cabin and the three of us were sat on one of the bunks with me in the middle. There was no use in trying to talk. I was gagged and the other two just sat there, like me, letting the enormity of what we had seen go through our minds. The other younger sailors, who, up till two days ago had been our friends were now required to stand guard over us on their own limited free time. That evening long after sunset some dinner was brought to the cabin and I was released. "Captain says that you are confined to your cabin for the duration of the voyage. We are not to talk to you and you are to sit on the bunk between meals." Looking at me he said, "And you are lucky that you are a passenger and not a crew member. Any crew member who tried to interfere with the captain would be flogged too." Chastened, all I could do was say "sorry," and Leonardo said, "We're sorry we got you in trouble. Is Alejandro OK?" "Alejandro will live, but have scars the rest of his life. The rest of us have lost our free time and have to stand guard outside your door. We are to learn that we are seamen and not passengers. Fortunately only Alejandro was flogged."

We passed another week at sea in the cabin. By day we were limited to sitting on the bunk in silence and the occasional whispered conversation. Nobody talked to us since the night of the flogging, I assume, having been warned of the consequences if caught talking to us. I spent time in thought. As far as I was concerned Alejandro was punished for no reason, and by extension, us also. I grew hard and in the daydreams of my mind I thought of how I would punish everyone who had wronged me. The captain, the brothers of Sylvia who had abused me and thrown me from the window leaving me to walk home naked. The best revenge I decided, was to become rich. If I were rich I would do what I wanted. By the time we docked in Santiago we were all three anxious to get ashore. "We will get together now in Santiago," we all promised, knowing that we probably would never see each other again. "We've gone through a lot together," agreed Gabriel. "We will be very busy in the new world." Said the very practical Leonardo. As we went down the gangplank we saw Alejandro working across the deck. He looked up at us, and then quickly looked down.

I walked through the dock and decided that I should make myself known to my uncle before heading to the plantations. All I knew is that it might take part of the day to get to the plantation so I might have to spend a couple days with my aunt and uncle before moving on. I knew, at least, after a week of sitting on the bunk that I would welcome any conversation. My heart grew lighter as I left the docks. Here I would be in charge and wouldn't have to worry about any captain holding rules over my head. Abruptly I changed course and walked the street facing the docks. Any street near the docks would have brothels. After six weeks of celibacy I was going to search out some entertainment before I met my uncle. Here I was in charge.

My afternoon of pleasure turned to night as I stayed at the brothel and took out my frustrations on several girls. I imagined the captain and Sylvia's brothers tied up and forced to watch while I ravaged every girl in the brothel in between flicking them with the whip. Beer and rum fueled my imagination.

The next morning I awoke with a terrific hangover and vomited in the slop bucket. I felt sick, but the sickness was so worth it after the weeks at sea. I cleaned myself up and prepared myself to visit my uncle. I didn't know how my uncle would treat me. I hardly remember him, and I'm sure I would just be a minor point in his day. Some few minutes between breakfast and lunch. Nevertheless I felt empowered by my night of pleasure. As I had become master of the girls last night, in my mind, I would become master of those around me. I left the brothel with a smile on my face. I was ready to face the world and ready to meet my uncle. I would become rich and powerful here in Cuba and I would find a way to the new world and become rich and powerful there.

I arrived at the governor's palace and presented myself at the office. My uncle would have received word I was coming, but not when so my arrival was not expected. "The governor will see you now," an aide said in the outer office. "Esteban," My uncle greeted me from the door, "Your aunt and I wondered if you had arrived on the ship yesterday. Did you have a good voyage?" I thought back through the voyage and lied. "Yes sir. We arrived yesterday and I spent last night with new friends here in Santiago. I didn't want to bother you with lodging last night." With a laugh my aunt entered the room, and with a kiss to my cheek, "Nonsense. You will spend today with us before heading out to the plantation tomorrow or the next day." My uncle looked like that was the last thing he wanted me to do, but smiled and said, "Yes. You will stay here. You have a home here in Santiago." I knew that that was said without excitement and knew that I would never spend another night here after tonight. "Well Señora, Esteban and I have much to discuss. We will see you for the comida."

My aunt left the office and my uncle invited me to sit, "So tell me about the family. Everyone is fine?" I answered truthfully that everyone was fine and sent their greetings. Then came the question I was expecting. "And you? Has your father sent you here to relieve him of problems if you stayed home?" Since I was expecting the question and I assumed he already knew the answer I answered in the affirmative, "My father thinks that I need some time away from Spain to grow up. I don't believe he wants me to embarrass the family name with certain indiscretions." My uncle smiled at my use of words and was blunt in his reply, "Indiscretion is true. From what I understand you have a hard time keeping your cock in your trousers." I blushed at his bluntness, and he continued, "You can just as easily embarrass yourself and the family here with many women. My suggestion its that you limit yourself to the brothels at the waterfront as you did last night." If I was shocked at his bluntness I was doubly shocked that he knew where I had spent the night. "Uncle, Sir. I hardly think I need to be spied upon. I'm not a child that needs to be watched every moment." He replied harshly, "Oh settle down. What kind of governor would I be if I didn't keep track of the island? What kind of uncle would I be if I didn't send somebody down to docks to check on the only ship coming in from Spain yesterday? Of course I knew your whereabouts and if you think you can fuck any woman or whore here with impunity you are mistaken. It's not that big an island that people don't know what's going on and talk about it." I started to feel boxed in and attacked with, "I'm not going to embarrass my father, or you." I finished with emphasis. "Good. Then we are understood. Now I think your aunt is expecting us for the comida after which you will accompany her on a drive around town so she can show you this sights. This evening's dinner will be a simple dinner with friends to welcome you to Cuba. You will say nothing of our conversation to your aunt. I do not wish her upset. Tomorrow morning after breakfast you will make your apologies to your aunt and tell her you are anxious to get to the plantation and take up your responsibilities." I muttered, "I'm so glad you have my life planned here." "What did you say?" came the quick and angry reply. "Yes sir. Thank you for you concern about my welfare." A tight smile and "That's what I thought you said. Come now.

Let's not keep your aunt waiting. She misses having family here to spoil." We walked down the hall from his office to the family area. Inside I was fuming at the way I was treated. If I had gold I would have power and not be bound by my uncle's rules.

Comida was ready by the time we got to the dining room. My aunt was happy to see me, "After comida and a short siesta we will go out riding so I can show you the city. Tonight we will have some friends for dinner so you can meet them." It was a relatively painless evening with my aunt chattering away and my uncle all smiles.

The next morning my aunt was bubbling with happiness, "Today I think I will show you more of the city. We hardly had time enough yesterday." Remembering my uncle's admonitions I said, "Thank you tia, but I'm afraid I must continue on to the plantation. I'm anxious to start my work there." My aunt looked surprised and a little upset, but my uncle interjected, "Yes dear. Esteban has much to do. He can come here often to be spoiled by you. Won't you Esteban?" Knowing what was expected of me I replied, "Yes auntie. I will come here often, but I must go on now. Please forgive me." Quickly she regained her composure. "Of course dear. You must be anxious to start. You're young and ready to take on the world." She and my uncle escorted me to the door with directions of how to arrange a horse and wagon to get to the plantation. My uncle shook my hand as I left. "Come visit often. There's always room for family." I left angry and determined to not visit again unless forced to.

Santiago was easy to navigate and I found somebody who was taking a wagon of supplies in the direction of the plantation, "From there it's an easy walk and you can call for your luggage later señor." It took most of the morning to get close to the plantation, "Señor. I'm turning off here, but your plantation is just up this road a 45 minute or hour walk. You'll be there soon." I walked up the road thinking of how I would manage the fields. Obviously I needed to learn how to manage the fields if I wanted to become rich. I vowed to make as much money as I could.

The estate manager Jose greeted me as I walked through the plantation. "Ah Señor, I wondered if you would be coming soon. I received a letter from your father a month ago so I assumed you would be coming on one of the next few ships." Jose was probably a little younger than my father, but not as uptight. I immediately liked him. "I'll send somebody to town in the next several days to collect your luggage and the supplies your father sent. With a wagon it takes the day to go to town and return, but with a horse you can make it to town in a couple hours. You'll want to visit your uncle often I'm sure. Not to worry. We take good care of the plantation here. You'll be able to visit your uncle as often as you want." Without telling Jose about my uncle's words I thanked him for the thoughts. "I'm sure I'll be going in to Santiago often," leaving out any mention of my uncle.

The next morning I woke a little unsure of where I was. I was no longer in Spain or at sea, and then I remembered that I was on the plantation. I lay for a moment thinking of what to do. My father certainly had succeeded if his goal was to place me far from temptations. The meal last night had been something simple that Jose's wife, one of the few women on the plantation, had prepared. There had been no rum or beer, "We don't think we need any here señor," Jose had said, "we live quietly and simply." So it looked as if I would be celibate and sober for the time being. "Ah good morning señor," said Jose as I explored the house, my new home. "I hope you slept well. We have been up working since daybreak to get the majority of the work done before it gets too hot." Not only was I to be celibate and sober it now looked like I would be rising early and taking my siesta after a wine free comida. "I sent one of the men to town with a wagon to collect your luggage and supplies from Spain." Continued Jose, "When you want to go to town to visit your uncle I'll set you up with a horse. It will be much faster than a wagon. You can ride a horse can't you?" I thought of what I had here versus what I could find in Santiago and knew that even if I didn't know how to ride a horse I could learn quickly to escape. "Well señor, here is a simple breakfast and we can be off and I'll show you your plantation." For the rest of the day we rode the plantation, with only occasional stops for water or to talk with the workers. I did try to be mature and learn some that day. If I wanted to be rich I would have to learn this. I was impressed by Jose's skills and knowledge. I couldn't remember what father had said about him, but I knew I could learn a lot.

That evening after sunset when we were having our light dinner before bed, since we had had the largest meal of the day at comida, I heard the creak of wagon wheels. "Ah. It's Felipe with the supplies," said Jose. "He must have gotten held up in town to arrive so late. We'll see how it went with him and unload supplies tomorrow." With that he was off to the wagon. I looked at my wine free meal and followed. "Señor Jose, Don Esteban," said the man driving the wagon. "Was there a problem in town?" asked Jose. "Why did it take so long. Usually you're back long before now." "Si Señor," answered Jose. "Usually I am back long before now. I went to the docks to collect Don Esteban's luggage and other supplies from Spain. When I got to the ship it was surrounded by the governor's guards and soldiers." My meal forgotten I hung on to every word. "What happened?" I asked. "I was stuck at the ship for most of the morning. They wouldn't let anyone enter or leave after I got there. I had to wait for the supplies anyway." Jose, obviously used to Felipe's method of storytelling, prompted, "Why were the soldiers there?" Felipe looked at him like he didn't understand, "why to search for the murderer, of course." I nearly shouted, but Jose held my arm, "Felipe why don't you start from there. Who was murdered?"

After many questions and interruptions I finally pieced together what had happened. "The captain was found dead in his cabin of a stab wound. The guards and soldiers were called since everything happened in port. The governor even came by." Felipe said, nodding at me when he mentioned the governor. "It was about this time that I got there and the governor," another nod in my direction as if to say what happened next was not his fault, "ordered nobody to go in our out of the docks, so I was held there for most of the day. The governor ordered the crew assembled on deck and everyone was there except one man who had been flogged just last week," I caught myself with a sharp intake of breath. "That man was missing and they think he did it." Jose looked at me, "Señor. Did you know that man? Why was he flogged?" Felipe answered for me, "He was a thief Don Jose, he was caught by the captain and ordered flogged. Obviously he killed the captain in port and escaped." I felt the world sink around me. I barely heard Felipe say, "The governor ordered all ships to be searched for the man and the guard was checking everybody leaving the city. I think he's escaped into the central mountains in hope of making it to Havana or elsewhere. I thought of my uncle's words "It's not that big an island that people won't know what you're doing." I wondered how Alejandro would survive in the mountains. Then I wondered if he might blame me for his flogging and try to find me. As if reading my mind, or knowing more than he was letting on, Jose said, "OK. We will put on guards around the plantation. If this man comes here we will catch him. All able bodied men will spend some time guarding after their shifts for the time being. Felipe, come in and get some dinner. You've had a long day."

With the excitement over for the time being I returned to my now cold meal and thought. If Alejandro did kill the captain why did he do it? True, I had probably fantasized about killing the captain during that last week sitting on the bunk, but I wouldn't have done it. I suppose that Alejandro would have been angry enough at the captain to kill him. After all, it was a joke that had gone bad. The obvious question then was Alejandro mad at me too for making him part of the failed joke? If he was angry, then was he on his way here to get even with me too? He knew my name and my family name. It wouldn't take much to know that my uncle was the governor and without too many questions he could find out where the plantation was. My thoughts were interrupted by Jose saying, "Señor we will have extra guards around the plantation. I don't think he would come this far away from town, he'll probably try to get to Havana or some other city where he's not known and get off the island that way. The longer he stays on the island the more time your uncle has to get the word out to the whole island." I thought for a moment. It sounded like Jose knew nothing about why Alejandro was flogged, or even that I had been at the whorehouse the first night I had been in town. I wouldn't have put it past my uncle to tell him that. "Jose, I think I should tell you something." I told him about the joke and how the captain had caught Alejandro with the money in hand. I also told him how I had tried to interrupt the punishment only to be restricted to the cabin for the remainder of the voyage. "So now I don't know if he could be running after me and blaming me for the flogging." Jose paused for a moment. "Well señor. Do not blame yourself for the flogging. The captain had more experience with the man than you did. If he was able to cut the cord that held the bag around Leonardo's neck without him knowing he was probably experienced at thievery. The captain might have seen that and decided he had had enough. He might have decided that he had found who had stolen something else and decided to make an example of him. True. It was a joke, but that's the way of life." He laughed, "Sounds like he made an example of you three too so the sailors would work harder." It was my turn to laugh, "I guess so, but I can't help but think it's still all my fault and Alejandro will come after me." Jose looked at me. "I think it's time you learn how to defend yourself. I imagine that you haven't had to use a musket yet?" I replied that that was true. "I also imagine that you haven't fought with a knife?" That was true. I was now 17 years old and hadn't been in too many fights, and none with a knife. "I guess as long as I'm being honest I'll tell you about my last fight that didn't end well." I told him about Sylvia and her brothers beating up on me and throwing me out the window." Jose laughed, "Well, you probably deserved that one, but I'm talking about protecting yourself in a fight. Starting tomorrow we are going to teach you shooting skills and knife fighting skills. If Alejandro comes here I want you prepared. Don't worry. I won't tell the men about Sylvia and her brothers, although they would think it pretty funny. I'll just tell them that you haven't had much training coming from the city. They'll believe that. They'll also appreciate help in guard duty. "

For the next several weeks I received daily lessons in shooting and fighting. I enjoyed my time with the men, some of whom were my age. At first we were all a little on edge thinking that Alejandro might try to come here to seek revenge, but as time passed the thought faded and I concentrated on improving my knife skills, "Señor you need to be able to strike with either hand. Keep your enemy guessing," said Felipe, who turned out to be a good fighter, as he showed me how to throw my knife between hands. "Do it without looking at the knife. Don't let him know what you are going to do." After about a month we cut down on the guard duty, "I think Alejandro is long gone to Havana and beyond or dead in the mountains," said Jose. "It's hard to survive without help and he wouldn't be staying in Santiago with everybody looking for him."

I relaxed at the thought and for the first time since I arrived on the plantation I decided to go back to town. "I think it's safe enough to go back now," I told Jose. "I might visit my uncle or my friends from the ship." "Yes," agreed Jose. "There's plenty of entertainment in Santiago!" he concluded with a knowing smile. I didn't tell him that I had no plans to visit my uncle. I didn't want to go through another session with him questioning everything I did. I'm sure with the stabbing he would have heard everything about the voyage. Somehow I didn't think that my offering to be flogged instead of Alejandro would raise his opinion of me. He would ask why I had behaved so poorly on the ship. No. I wouldn't be going to the palace. My destination was a few blocks away near the waterfront.

My thoughts returned to my uncle's office as I tried to pay attention to what he was saying. My uncle is governor of Cuba and as such he controls any voyages of exploration out of Cuba. By getting in good with him as soon as I was exiled here to Cuba I assured myself of a spot in any voyages of exploration to the new world. This assures me a portion of treasure discovered in the new world. Actually I might be able to get a double portion of gold if I worked it just right. As the governor's nephew and his ears on board the ship I could ask for a portion of the governor's share of the treasure. As a member of the voyage of discovery I could claim a share of the treasure too. Of course this share would be after the King's Fifth, that fifth part of any treasure that by law goes to the king. I know the way bookkeeping works. The King, of course, will get his fifth. No captain dares to slight the king in anything. The governor will get his fifth, which is where I hope to get the first part of my return on investment. My uncle will need to pay me for being his ears on the voyage. After the King and governor take their shares the captain will split up the rest and this is where creative bookkeeping comes in. The captain must pay the cost of the voyage such as food, weapons, sails and anything associated with the voyage. Sometimes money can be made with two sets of books. If lucky I can be made bookkeeper for the voyage. I could create two sets of books. One book to show the King and Governor and another to share with the captain. I suppose I could try creating three sets of books with one just for me. I could try that but I don't relish the idea of being caught with three sets of books and the ensuing problems that would create. Problems! If caught embezzling from the voyage the captain wouldn't have any qualms about killing me. Probably by hanging after whipping my bare back in front of all the crew as a warning.

"Do you think you can do that," questioned my uncle." I was quickly brought back to the conversation in his office. "Yes Sir. I think I can convince Cortez that I am estranged from you." That part would be easy. Although he was my uncle I wasn't that close to him. I doubt he even knew that Cortez and I already knew each other.

Cortez is Hernan Cortez another young man from Spain. I suppose we are somewhat alike. We both yearn for adventure and we both, perhaps, have been sent here to grow up and learn about the family business interests.

50

Cortez is a few years older than I, maybe 29 to my 18, so we aren't close friends. From the stories I have heard about him I think he might have been sent here to keep from embarrassing the family name. One story is that he had to escape naked out the window of a married woman's bedroom ahead of her husband. I've heard stories that happened in Spain before he came here, but then I've also heard it happened here too. Cortez is married now but I don't think he minds the stories. He and I were drinking with a group of mutual friends when somebody drunkenly made suggestions of married women and naked escapes. "Ha! You've heard of that too!" Was the beery answer. If upset he didn't show it. "Well if I lead a voyage of discovery we shall see if the women of the new world are as beautiful as the women of Spain! Or Cuba," he continued with his eyes on the tavern serving maid.

When I arrived in Cuba I knew that I had to get to the new world and seek my adventure and gold. I would not be happy on my father's fields keeping books and making nice with the estate managers. I wanted adventure and I sought out those who could help me achieve it. I met Cortez within the first few weeks I was in Cuba, after the worries about Alejandro died down. My father''s fields were several leagues out of Santiago but I spent little time there. Although I was supposed to learn to manage the fields and people I was far from my father's control and the estate managers could and had done everything without me. I spent time in the bars of Santiago picking up new friends with the help of my father's purse and easy beer. "If you want to go to the new world on an expedition," one of the sailors said, "you've got to find Cortez." "Who's that?" I asked. "He's from Spain. He's already been on expeditions around the area. He's like you: seeking adventure." With that I was out looking for him over the next few weeks. I had to spend some time in the fields learning from the estate manager but left word in Santiago that I would like to meet Cortez. While I waited I tried to learn from the estate manager. Jose was a Spaniard, a former sailor no longer able to sail, who had to take up other work. "The fields are like the ship." He said. "You've got to manage the people and anything can happen." He taught me about the field work that they did here. I found it was as boring as when my father tried to teach me the same thing in Spain. Jose also showed me how to keep the books for the estates. "We keep the books accurate, but we don't tell your uncle everything, sometimes we have to make 'donations' to his accountants and representatives" he said with a smile. It was there I got the idea that would cause problems in the future. To my surprise I rather enjoyed keeping books. I enjoyed watching the numbers float on the page and I dreamed of the gold each number represented. I enjoyed thinking how I could keep those numbers on my side of the ledger. It was during that time that I got word from Santiago that Cortez was back in town. I set out as soon as I could disentangle myself from the fields and books. It wasn't hard to find Cortez and introduce myself in a bar where I bought the first round. "I want to go on a voyage of discovery," I said. "I want to see the new world." Cortez laughed. "It's not as glamorous as you think, but it's an adventure. Tell me about yourself." I opened up to him about my past and how my father had sent me here to learn responsibility and to keep me away from the upper class women of Segovia. "Ha! We are a lot alike." He laughed as he called for another beer with a slap to the serving girl's rump. He told me about jumping naked out of a married woman's window. Then it was my turn to laugh as I told him about Juan and I, "We found our clothes in the bushes under the window and slunk away hoping that we wouldn't be caught." Cortez laughed, "And so you ended up here! Cuba is a good place and the life here is easy. Certainly the Cuban winter can't compare to Spain. Why don't you stay here and learn what you can to go back to make yourself a name at court?" I agreed that eventually I would have to return to Spain, but for now I wanted to see the new world. "Well. I don't have an expedition going now so I can't help you. If you hear of anything let me know." Then he paused, "did you say your surname is Velazquez? The Velazquez?" I had to admit who my uncle was, "But if you think my last name can help you get a ship you're wrong. My uncle met me when I landed here and that has been it. I think my reputation hasn't helped." He took another swig of his beer. "Well it's good to have friends whatever their name is. We will keep in touch and

I'll introduce you around the area." And so we became friends. I went back and forth between the fields and Santiago as often as I could. I learned that Cortez probably had more access to my uncle than I did. He was well known in the government as an able administrator and treasurer. He was devout in his faith, saying his devotions in the morning, but meeting friends in the evening. He was a strong leader with great ambitions. With great ambitions came a headstrong will to succeed. He was popular in the government but difficult to control.

"Cortez," said Jose when I was back to the fields. "He's a strong leader. If anyone can command an expedition to the new world it would be him. Of course nobody can command Cortez except maybe the king, and even that's doubtful." He concluded with a laugh. "If you can learn to motivate men like he does you will go far, but beware if you cross him or you will pay the price." I heard the first part of the sentence, but ignored the second part. An omission I would come to regret. I took a more active role in managing the fields trying to learn at least Jose's ability to lead people. I also learned more about bookkeeping, eventually surpassing the abilities of Jose. "I've taught you all I can about accounting." He said. "You will make your father proud in what you have learned." I smiled at the praise. In truth I did enjoy the bookkeeping, and if I hadn't been so intent on going on an expedition I would truly have made my father happy. But to go on an expedition required money and my new found expertise in accounting provided me with an idea. I could keep two books. One book I would show Jose, my father, and the representatives of my uncle. These representatives would always accept the records as long as the appropriate incentive was given. This incentive was identified in my second book as a donation. The second book kept me in beer money to lubricate my network of friends, Cortez included, who could help me get a position on an expedition. "Your uncle is planning an expedition. He wants to make trading trips to the west. If I can get command of that expedition I can take you on if you can invest in the expedition." That brought up how these voyages of discovery worked. They all required money. Money in the form of an investment in hope of a golden return. Even Colon had to get financial backing from the king and queen of Spain. Of course, for them, the return paid off handsomely. Not every investor could, or wanted to go on the expedition, but I was young and able and perhaps I could get onboard. "Do you think you have access to your uncle?" I had to admit that I had no access to my uncle. "I still haven't seen him since he briefly met me when I arrived. I think you have more access than I." He grunted, "Well it was worth a try."

I went back to the fields to work and keep track of my two sets of books. I was somewhat surprised the following week when I received word that my uncle wished to see me. I had no idea why and my first thought was that something had happened to my father and I would have to go home to take up his place as head of the family and position at court. I was greeted at the governor's palace by my aunt, "Tia," I said. "So good to see you. Are you well? Is there news about my father? Has something happened?" Surprised at my thought she said, "Oh no. Your father is fine. Did you think something had happened and that's why Diego called you?" I gave an inward sigh of relief as she continued, "Everything is fine with your father. We just received a letter several days ago. I don't know why he wants to see you, but he's waiting for you in his office. Go. We will talk over dinner later."

And so I was ushered in to my uncle's office where he laid out his plan and my mind began to work out my plan. His plan was relatively simple. He needed a strong commander to lead an expedition of trade to the new world. It had to be an expedition of trade and not conquest because an expedition of conquest would result in the money being split between the king and vice regent of the new world. That would cut my uncle out of any return. In a trade expedition the governor could claim a fifth and the king a fifth. The other investors could take what was left. My uncle craved power and money but needed me to get it. "I need you to be my eyes and ears on the expedition. Cortez is a strong commander, but I need to know if he is withholding things from me. If you can do that you will be richly rewarded and your father will be proud of you." My mind went wild with thoughts of how I could make this work to my benefit.

Yes. It will be difficult, but I think I can satisfy both Cortez and my uncle. Cortez knew nothing about this meeting with my uncle and my uncle knows nothing about my friendship with Cortez. My uncle's words brought me out of my reverie, "I shall be talking to him next week about making a voyage of discovery to the west. It would just be a voyage of discovery, not colonization, to see what lies to the west. If we can discover lands then we can talk about colonizing them for His Majesty." In truth I think my uncle is a little timid about exploration. He wants the glory, but I don't think he is willing to give up the good life he has here in Cuba. "After I do and he starts searching for a crew I want you to sign up as a crewman. I doubt he would believe you a sailor or soldier, but maybe you can convince him that you are an officer or adventurer." Glancing at my face he drilled to my very being. "That shouldn't be hard to do." My uncle might not be ready for an adventure, but he certainly can read people. "That shall be all for now. Give your father my best when you write him. I shall send word to you when I have talked to Cortez. From there it is your responsibility to become a member of the crew. We will go now and have dinner with your tia."

I left the governor's palace deep in thought. Yes. I think I could convince Cortez I would be of good use. He and I might be alike in our love of adventure, but he would need men besides soldiers and sailors. I might not be a good sailor but I should be able to convince him of my worth as accountant or scribe.

It didn't take long for Cortez and my uncle to meet. In the end it wasn't even difficult. My uncle wanted to send an exhibition to the West and Cortez wanted to lead one. The only difficult thing was arranging the words of the contract. My uncle wants a voyage of discovery and trade to bring back gold. I believe that Cortez wants to colonize anything he finds. I'm sure there will be some arguments about that, but I don't care. My plan is to get onboard the ship in search of adventure and gold.

Cortez put word out around the city of Santiago that he needed investors, soldiers, and sailors. Since I wasn't part of the later two I went to him about investing in the journey and going as a scribe. "Well. Bernal will be going as our scribe and soldier, but if you are managing your properties here in Cuba I could use you as an accountant and money manager. If you have the money to invest in the expedition you can join as long as you're willing to work. Of course everybody will have to be a soldier when needed." He threw that out as almost an afterthought. No matter. I had heard the magic word. He had said accountant and I knew that I could keep two sets of books to make my uncle and me both very rich. Since I was now an investor I had to come up with some money to invest in the expedition. I took money that I had saved from my two books and borrowed money against the family lands for the rest. I hoped that it would be repaid before my father found out. At the very least I knew that he wouldn't find out till I had already been on the expedition for a month and by that time I might be rich.

Cortez and I developed our friendship over time as we prepared for the expedition. We met regularly for beer and the occasional evening with those ladies who were willing to part with their virtue for money. Cortez might be able to carry on discrete relationships with women of the upper class, but I had nowhere near his status or charisma. I would have to settle for paying for my pleasure. "How is the money coming in for the expedition? Do we have enough to proceed" He questioned one day. Although he was an accountant and treasurer he had given me control of the expedition's books while he prepared everything else. "Yes. We have nearly enough to go and I think we will have ample money by the time we leave." I showed him the books of what we had brought in from the various investors and what we had spent for supplies, crew and everything relating to keeping a ship afloat.

As the time grew closer for departure I started to sense some misgivings on my uncle's part. I knew that he didn't want to give up the comforts of Cuba to go on this, but he didn't know how he was going to control Cortez and get his share of the treasure. This is where I decided to come clean and tell him that Cortez had asked me to be the accountant of the voyage. "If I am the accountant I will be able to make sure that you get your share of the treasure. I have done what you wanted and become friends with Cortez. He and I are very close and I'll make sure that you get your fifth." I didn't say anything about keeping two accounting books. That might be a common practice, but I wasn't going to advertise it to my uncle. Besides. If anybody was going to get rich from two accounting books it was going to be me. I had already planned out how I would keep the two books by showing more money for charges than what I had actually paid. Before we were even on our way I had managed to divert money to my own bank account without my uncle or Cortez finding out. "Fine." My uncle said. "I won't worry now if I know you are there to keep an eye on things." I wondered if he truly trusted me or had resigned himself to fate in this expedition.

On the night before we left my uncle came to the dock to see us off. There were flowery speeches about exploration and bringing the Church to the world. There were priests on board, but I paid no attention to them. I was concerned about the gold.

In January 1519 we set sail from Santiago en route for Havana. I think Cortez was worried that my uncle might change his mind and call off the expedition and wanted to put as much space between him and the governor as possible. We were several days at sea to Havana where we stopped for more provisions and water. During this time I had a chance to meet some of the men who would become part of my life. I've already talked some about Cortez. He is driven for success and wants to colonize these new lands to make a name for himself in Spain. He wants lands and titles and will settle for nothing less. Though my uncle wants me to be his eyes and ears I am immediately drawn in to his magnetism. I get the feeling that if he would ask his soldiers and sailors to walk across the country for him they would. Little did I know how true these thoughts would become.

Another man who was destined to become part of my life was Bernal. He was the self appointed scribe of the voyage. He always seemed to have a quill in hand to record his thoughts. "Some day I will write all this down." Since I was the expedition's accountant I was given berth in a cabin with two other junior officers. They were young men from Spain who had sailed with Cortez on a previous expedition. Santiago and Mateo were friends from Seville of upper class families who had fallen on hard times. Together they had left Seville for Cuba to manage fields there for absentee landlords. Although capable young men they were forced to leave the fields when the Spanish owners sent family members to manage their fields. They had joined other expeditions as midshipmen and learned the skills they were now performing as junior officers. The three of us considered ourselves fortunate to be on the expedition and to have a cabin, although small, for our own. The cabin consisted of bunk bed on one side of the cabin with another bunk above a work area where I kept the books and Mateo, being the navigator kept his sextant and charts. Santiago, as an officer, was kept busy with security and maintaining ship discipline. We were all busy during the day and Mateo checking his charts at night with the help of the stars. Now on our first time out on our way to Havana we had time to talk. We told our stories and dreams. "I consider myself fortunate," said Mateo. "I've learnt navigation since I left Spain. This will keep me employed on any ship. On this trip we can share in the treasure and I will someday be able to return home and help restore our family name." I thought that if I came home with enough money I would make my father proud that I bore the family name. Santiago continued with his dreams, "If I work hard as an officer now I could advance and stay at sea. Now that we are exploring the new world there will always be ships between Spain and the new world. Someday I'll have my own command." He concluded to our laughs. I went to my bunk above the work area that night content with friends and how my life was turning out. Someday I could return home with gold and my father would be proud.

The night before we landed in Havana Cortez called me to his cabin. "Tomorrow we dock in Havana to take on supplies and do the rest of the preparations. I will be meeting with as many of the wealthy of the city to talk about investing in the expedition. I want you to make arrangements with a bank to take their investments to set against the loans I pulled out in Santiago. I also want to buy as much as we can here to trade with the natives." I agreed that I would search out a banker as soon as we landed and told him I would take care of everything.

"Don't worry," I concluded, "we will have enough money to make this a successful voyage." I didn't add that it was already a successful voyage for me. "Yes," he said, pouring us each a glass of wine, "I'm glad we met each other, how long has it been? Almost two years ago? We've become good friends and I'm glad I can trust you." We sat there in companionable silence with our wine each thinking our thoughts. "I think you have a great future ahead of you," remarked the older Cortez. "You have brains and if we do everything right on this voyage you will have money." With the thought of my second book in mind I replied, "I hope we all become rich."

In Havana we spent some time taking on supplies and Cortez talking up the mission with the local leaders. Santiago and Mateo were kept busy on the ship while I went ashore with Cortez to do our work. Here is where I saw again the strength of Cortez' personality. He set himself up in the house of the mayor and received visitors each day. My friendship with Cortez had worked well as I set myself up with him, as I told him, "to receive any investments from the caudillos and pay for supplies." If Cortez suspected that I was keeping an eye out for my uncle he didn't say anything. The visitors came and Cortez enthralled them with stories of what they might find to the west. True. We did have some idea of what lay beyond. Stories had come from a previous expedition of people dressed in feathers and loin cloths. The stories told of jewels and gold taken as gifts from the natives. Cortez told of how he would bring gold back from what he called "This land of the Mexica and you shall be rich as well as the whole island of Cuba". The local leaders of Havana believed it and I had a line of people ready to invest in the project.

Then word came from Santiago that my uncle had finally decided that he could not trust Cortez. He ordered the local authorities to arrest Cortez and call off the expedition. I was worried that I might have to show support for my uncle or give up the project that I had borrowed against my father's land. As it was I shouldn't have worried. The mayor made it clear that he was not going to arrest Cortez and the line of men ready to invest in the project became longer. With Santiago being far from Havana any further attempt by my uncle to stop Cortez would take weeks of overland travel. With the new investors I was soon able to add to my second book and with the help of a discrete banker I was able to pay off my loan and send money back to Santiago. Cortez was pleased with the investments, "You've done a great job keeping care of the books. Everyone I talk to tells me how easy it is to work with you and how well you work with the men here and the crew. I'm proud of what you've done so far on this expedition and although you are not an officer you are a vital member of the crew and my good friend." I blushed at the compliment, "I'm proud to be part of this expedition, but even prouder to be called your friend." That part was true. I was proud to be both a friend of

Cortez and part of this expedition. The truth that I was stealing from the project never entered my mind. In my mind it was simply a challenge to be conquered as Cortez considered my uncle a challenge to be controlled. Cortez sent a flowery letter to my uncle about the riches they would soon see and the greatness of the project. Whether my uncle believed this letter when he received it I wouldn't know because after he sent the letter Cortez wasted no time in preparing the ships for immediate departure. Cortez stopped by our small cabin and told Mateo to be prepared for departure with his charts and looking at me, "We will leave before the governor gets any more ideas."

Mexica

Esteban speaks

On February 10, 1519 we set sail from Havana in search of the land of the Mexica. The ships were loaded with cannon, arms, and ammunition. There were just over 600 men ready to search for riches.

After some days at sea we saw land in the distance. Cortez ordered that we sail along the coast to determine the best possible place to put ashore. We then discovered an island off the coast and Cortez decided to drop anchor there and go ashore. "Esteban, I want you to come ashore with us." Cortez said, "You should see what we've been searching for." Mateo and Santiago were also on that first landing in the new world. I was excited that at last I would see the new world and maybe find gold right away. As we came ashore in our small boats we saw natives waiting for us. I remembered that the previous expedition said that the natives fled at the sight of the ships so these people must have been used to seeing white men and their large ships. Natives were waiting for us, but of course could not understand us. "I've heard stories of shipwrecks around here," said Cortez, "I wonder if there were any survivors." The natives listened to our speaking and several of them seemed to talk amongst themselves and suddenly one of the younger men raced away from the beach heading to a settlement some distance inland and up the shore. Not knowing what was happening we watched as the sailors continued to load barrels of water into the boats to take them back to the ship. Cortez had some trinkets and beads that he brought out of his pocket to give to some of the natives. With nothing better to do Mateo, Santiago and I walked up the shore a little to see what discoveries we could make in this new world. We were walking up the shore in the general direction of where the young man had run from the group of natives when I saw somebody returning through the brush. At first I didn't pay too much attention. I suppose if I had been terribly concerned about violence or if I knew then what I know now I would never have left where Cortez was with the others. I felt safe with my two friends. Suddenly I heard a shout, "Jesus, Mary, and Joseph! Are you Spanish?" and I saw a sun bronzed man with long gray hair emerge from the brush. "You are! Tell me. Is it Wednesday?" he asked, pulling a prayer book from his pocket. "I've been praying for rescue. I've counted the days since I was ship wrecked." I was astounded, but quickly regained my composure. "Yes. You are ok now. You have been rescued. Hernan Cortez is here with ships on a voyage of discovery." By now we were nearly back to the ship party and Cortez looked both surprised and delighted to see the man. "Oh. Thank God and the Virgin! I have been rescued!" and the man started crying. "I've been waiting and counting the days in my prayer book," he said again. Cortez ordered food, water, and beer be brought to the man. "You are safe now sir. Tell us your story."

The man took a swig of beer, "My name is Fr. Geronimo de Aguilar and I was shipwrecked in 1511. Our ship wrecked off the coast and any survivors were captured." He shuddered as if not wanting to remember. "It was terrible. We were kept in cages and brought out one by one. I could see and hear everything: it was terrible." We were all enthralled by the story even though afraid of what we would hear next. "They would drag out a man naked from the cage. It didn't matter if he were Spanish or a native. The man would be stretched across a stone with men holding arms and legs. A priest then took a stone blade and dove it in to the man's chest and ripped out his still beating heart." Aguilar broke down in tears again, "I heard the screams of my friends as they died and I could do nothing. This went on for weeks. Some days they would take one person and some days two or more." We stood there in shock. Some men turned white. Others looked like they wanted to throw up. I felt sick fear. "The priest would take the heart and throw it in a fire burning nearby. They were sacrificing God fearing Spaniards to some pagan god," he concluded with more tears. Cortez let him cry for a moment. "You are safe now Fr. Aguilar. We will protect you, but tell us. How did you escape?" Aguilar calmed down as if the worst part of the story was over. "Yes," he said, almost as if he just realized it, "I escaped.

As I said this went on for weeks. As time went on and there were fewer men in the cages the natives spent less time guarding us. I was able to loosen the ropes connecting the wooden bars of the cage enough that I was able to escape with another sailor. We were captured again, but this time by the Maya and have been held as slaves since then." Turning he spoke something in the native language and another young man turned and left the shore at a run toward the village. It was Cortez' turn to look surprised. "You speak the language? There's another one of you?" Aguilar took another swig of beer with a smile on his face. "Yes. I sent for him now. I don't think he'll want to leave. He's taken a woman here." Cortez smiled, "I think you will be a very valuable part of our expedition if you can speak the language." At that moment we heard a rustle in the brush around the beach and another white man bronzed dark from the sun emerged. "Here is Guerrero," stated the newly found priest. "Perhaps you can persuade him to come too." Guerrero turned out to not be as willing to leave as Fr. Aguilar. "I have a woman and children here now. What do I have in Spain?" he announced forcefully. Cortez pondered for a moment, "We will be here for a few more days. If you change your mind just come to the shore and wave and we will come for you." Guerrero was as determined to stay as Aguilar was to go. "I have my wife," was all he said. "I'm not leaving her. Aguilar hadn't forsaken his vows all the time that he was a captive. "I took a vow when I became a priest and I didn't renounce it,," he declared. "If you have no priest onboard I shall celebrate mass." We stayed near the island for several days before setting sail again for the frontier of the Maya country. Guerrero stayed onshore and watched us as we left. No words from Cortez or Aguilar could persuade him to leave.

As we set sail for the land of the Maya Cortez laid out his plan. Again he called me to his cabin to take me into his confidence, "We are going to colonize this new world in the name of King Charles. We will set up camp and learn as much as we can, but we won't stop at just simple trade." As I thought, this was not going to be a journey of trade. Cortez meant to colonize the Mexica or Maya in the name of King Charles. I noticed without saying anything that he left out any mention of my uncle. I began to wonder who I was going to have to show my allegiance to. For now my two books were safely hidden and since I had no way to return to Cuba my lot was with Cortez. After several several days at sea we saw the mouth of a river in the distance and Cortez gave the order to move nearby so we could provision the ships. Upon inspection of the riverbank we saw it full of native soldiers with all types of weapons. Here is where Aguilar proved his value to our expedition. Cortez sent him with several officers on one of the boats to ask permission to land. It was a short trip to shore and back. Aguilar returned and said, "They refused any of our requests to come ashore and provision the ships." Cortez just grunted a reply, "We will take it then."

70

He ordered the ships to set back some so that anybody on shore would think that we were leaving and then as the sun set he went onshore with several soldiers and officers. I did not go with them as I was not considered a soldier. They were gone several hours and sometime in the middle of the night they returned. The next morning all were rousted out of hammocks early as we made ready for battle. Cortez had spent the night exploring the area and had come up with a plan. Soldiers were ferried to shore and cannon loaded on boats and even the horses were freed from their confinement aboard ship. I'll admit to being nervous, excited and afraid all at the same time. Since I've already admitted to not being a soldier I was assigned to a boat to help with a cannon. Mateo was in the boat with me while Santiago as more of a soldier commanded another boat. We worked our way close to shore firing the cannon, which I'm sure had never been seen by the natives before. The soldiers worked their way inland toward the city and soon the horses and riders were sent out too. If the cannon didn't scare the enemy I'm sure that the horses did. I suppose if I had never seen a mounted soldier before I would think it was one huge animal. The fight was over and Cortez had gained his foothold in the land of the Mexica.

Except this was not the land of the Mexica. This was the land of the Tabasco. These people were of an extended tribe that lived close to shore. The next day the leaders of the Tabasco came to Cortez who had set himself up in the middle of the city that had just the day before been part of a battle. Cortez didn't greet them as a conquering general, but as a friend, "I come from a great king who desires to spread his protection over you and I bring you the good news of God and the Virgin Mary." He said all this through Aguilar who seemed very happy to be away from his slavery and back among Spaniards. The Tabasco didn't have a choice but to accept Charles V as their new sovereign, perhaps thinking that one master across the sea was the same as another master of a neighboring tribe. I was surprised when as part of the peace settlement twenty women were brought to Cortez. These women were the prizes of war. I had never really thought of that before. I might have been sent to Cuba to avoid embarrassing my father with my behavior, but I hadn't expected the prizes of war to include women. In Cuba there were certain women who volunteered their bodies in exchange for money so I hadn't sullied my father's reputation there. When these women were paraded in front of Cortez and crew I almost felt a sense of lust and hoped that my friendship with Cortez would get me a woman. As they left the protection of their people one of the women let out a cry before quickly being silenced by the elders. I realized that these women were daughters of the tribal chieftains being given over to Cortez in exchange for peace. I thought of my mother and sister at home. This is the way of the world and the way of war, but for a moment I felt ashamed of my role in it. Any sense of shame fell away as

Cortez called my name, "Esteban. Take this woman. Each of the captains and officers now have a woman for comfort and to cook and clean. Make sure you use her well." He concluded with a bawdy laugh. I left with the woman on my arm. She looked afraid and appeared much younger than my 18 years. No matter. I now had a woman that I didn't have to pay for. I couldn't take her to the cabin I shared with Mateo and Santiago, so I took her to some brush at the edge of the beach and had my way with her. With my needs met I pulled up my trousers and pointed at the ship. "You go there." I said fairly loudly even though I knew she couldn't understand me. She would have to find her own way onboard the ship and her own quarters once she got there. My use for her was cooking, cleaning and coupling. She looked at me with tears in her eyes, but a stoic look on her face. The kind of look women in her position have been giving conquerors for years. It was a look of resignation, mixed with hate. No matter. My needs were met and I had money in the bank. Soon I would be rich.

Vera Cruz

Tenochtitlan
Cuauhtémoc Speaks

The rumors are coming from the coast again and I find myself bowing before my cousin, "My lord Tlatoani what news do you hear from the coast?" Montezuma looked at me as though he knew that I already knew what he was about to say. "Yes. The white men have taken the Tabasco vassal tribe. They arrived in this One Reed Year and on Quetzalcoatl's name day. The head of the white men asks questions about us and the tribes between here and the sea. I believe they will want to come here, but I shall stall them. If this is Quetzalcoatl returning I cannot kill the head and must study more. They shall be held at the sea for now.

I returned to my house across the lake unsure. The signs might be there that this white man could be Quetzalcoatl returning, but my instincts tell me no. We have stories of Huitzilopochtli leading our ancestors, but we never hear of him taking the shape of a man. I caught myself thinking "if I were Tlatoani" and immediately regretted my thoughts against the order of things. But it was too late. In my mind I wouldn't let these men get closer to Tenochtitlan.

The Cortez Camp
Esteban speaks

We spent several days at sea leaving Tabasco area in search of the next area to land in search of treasure. On Good Friday, 1519 we anchored offshore and almost immediately saw canoes leaving shore. The men in the canoes waved at us and pointed to shore. If this was a trap it didn't look like it. The shores were clear and there was no sight of native soldiers. The canoes approached the ship and Cortez allowed them to board. Here the events surprised everybody. The natives came forward and spoke in a language that Aguilar did not understand, but from behind the crowd one of the native women stood up and pointed at Cortez. This woman understood the local language. Her name was Malinche, but since she had been offered as a peace prize she had since been Baptized as Marina. Malinche stood up and pointed at Cortez and then without asking permission from Cortez said something to Aguilar who then translated it to Spanish. "They want to know who the leader is." By lucky chance we now had a way to translate between us and the local natives. Through this method of communication we continued for a long time. Cortez introduced himself again as the representative of the great emperor Charles who wished to extend his protection. The locals replied that they were servants of another great emperor who lived some distance away. Cortez replied that he wished to journey to the land of the emperor to greet him as a representative of Charles. With that the locals looked a little worried and replied that it was a long journey from here and perhaps difficult. Cortez continued how he would love to meet the emperor and extend the greetings of Charles. It was politely refused again but this time Cortez invited them to return for the Easter celebration two days later.

Tenochtitlan
Cuauhtémoc Speaks

I visited the palace today on the pretext of asking my cousin if anything was new. In reality I know what my runners had reported to me and I'm sure was reported to Montezuma. "Yes. The white men have landed again. My people were sent with a captive to sacrifice and he refused to sacrifice him. They also offered food with sacrificial blood and was refused. I'm now more convinced than ever that this man is Quetzalcoatl returned. He refused to eat the sacrificial food and we know that Quetzalcoatl does not require sacrifice. If he comes here and demands the throne who am I to fight a god? I have instructed my people to keep him at the sea with gifts. If he receives all the gifts he might leave happy." I left again worried about Tenochtitlan. I didn't think that giving this white man gifts would satisfy him and he wouldn't be happy till he had come here in search of gold.

The Cortez Camp
Esteban Speaks

Easter Sunday dawned and we gathered at the beach to celebrate the Resurrection. Cortez himself read from the Bible, while the priests wore all the finery they had been able to carry onboard ship. The newly baptized women were allowed to take Communion since they were our newest Christians. My woman amongst them with the newly baptized name of Sarah. The native leaders were there and watched as captain and crew reverently kissed the cross. Later they brought food to us. Some of it had a foul smell of blood on it. Cortez refused it as disgusting and again was appalled when a man was brought forward and told by way of Aguilar and Malinche that they could sacrifice him to Cortez if he wished. When Cortez declined both the natives said nothing. Cortez again asked to go to see the emperor whom we now know lives in a city called Tenochtitlan. Again they murmured that it was a long difficult journey, but perhaps the great Cortez would like some gifts from one emperor to another. A huge feathered banner was brought out which I assumed represented a god. Then I saw what I had been waiting for: Gold. Gold jewelry and chains. Brilliant stones and more fine pieces of jewelry. I started mentally calculating the value in each of my books and how much would go to the king and how much to me.

The other crew stared at the gold. Even Cortez appeared shocked at the value of the gold in front of him. "I must go to Montezuma to give him thanks from my great emperor Charles." The native leaders again said how difficult that would be and how long the trip was, "There would be no way to get food," came the response from Malinche and Aguilar. Cortez put Santiago, as head of security, in charge of moving the treasure to the ships. I, as the accountant, was in charge of inventorying the treasure. As one bracelet went past our hands I repeated aloud what I was putting in the book, but didn't bother to write it down in the book. Mateo, several crewmen and I moved the gold to the ship's hold. As we were leaving the hold I saw the gold bracelet. I saw it and thought it would make a good addition to my personal treasure and not in the inventory. With nobody looking I grabbed it and continued my work. My two cabin mates and I worked for several hours and when we returned to the cabin I casually dropped the bracelet in to my bag while they weren't looking. Later that evening over a glass of wine Cortez shared how shocked he was at the amount of gold. Without thinking I said, "If we go home now we shall be rich." Cortez said nothing, but smiled at my outburst. When we went to bed that night after helping Mateo take our bearings with his sextant Santiago asked "How much do you think our share of that gold would be?" Mateo answered, "I don't know. You know we would be the last after the king, governor, investors and expenses. I think we would be lucky to get enough money to purchase a new sword. Isn't that right Esteban? You do the books." Yes. We wouldn't get much after paying all expenses. The king gets a fifth and the governor too." Smiling I thought of my second book and drifted off to sleep.

Tenochtitlan
Cuauhtémoc Speaks

The invaders are still there. My cousin still believes the leader to be Quetzalcoatl returned and has given them gifts in hopes that they will be happy and leave. My runners tell me they show no signs of leaving, but continually ask about coming to visit Montezuma and Tenochtitlan. My cousin ordered the local tribes to not give the invaders so much food. Perhaps if they are hungry they will leave and go back to where they came from. He has also ordered his magicians to cast spells on the entire group to force them to leave. I trust not these magicians. I trust the spears of my men. I wish to see this invader splayed out on the sacrificial stone in the temple.

The Cortez Camp
Esteban Speaks

It is hot here. Hot and humid and the air is full of mosquitos. Men are grumbling and wishing to go home or go on to the mountains. So far Cortez has kept the men happy with promises of the gold to come. After seeing the gold that we received from Montezuma I was happy to wait it out, but now I am starting to tire of this wait and lack of food. Some men want to go home, but Cortez tells them if they leave the king will lose this new colony. For several days he and other leaders not from Cuba had holed themselves up in his cabin talking and planning. I was a little hurt that I hadn't been invited to this group since I was accountant and friend. When I asked over wine one night what they were doing he said, "Oh nothing to do with money so that's why I didn't have you part of the group. We just need to plan where we will go next." I left happy with his response. It had nothing to do with money and since he was talking with captains I knew that he would be planning on how far up the coast to go. I assumed he would go up the coast more and maybe trade with other local tribes before heading back to Cuba. With luck in a few months I would be home in Cuba and rich. If luck held my father would be proud of my accomplishments and I would be allowed to return to Spain and take up my position there. My life was looking up.

We had some free time during these days so one morning early before the sun became too hot Santiago,

Mateo and I went on our own expedition down the beach. We walked for over an hour talking about our dreams and what we had so far accomplished on the expedition. "Look at the crops" I said. "It looks like home. This is a rich area." Mateo agreed. "It's beautiful here even though it's hot and humid. Look at the water. It's better than the beaches of home. I think we could go swimming here." Within a moment we had shed our clothes and were playing in the surf. "You could take your woman here and have her right on the beach," Santiago said. "We could all have her!" Mateo interrupted. "That's what friends are for! I laughed and dove for Santiago's legs to trip him in the surf. Santiago laughed and pushed me away and went deeper in the water. Suddenly he shouted as he seemed to move quickly away from us. He had gotten caught in a shore current and was being pulled away from us. "Don't swim against the current." Mateo shouted. "You'll tire yourself out. Swim with the current." Without thinking I grabbed one of our trousers that had been left on the ground as we stripped to go swimming. "Come Esteban. Mateo shouted. "We'll catch him up the beach." We ran up the beach and waded out as far as we could. "Hold my hand," Mateo ordered, "and I'll throw him the trousers." We were out as far as we could go and I planted my feet firmly in the sand and held out my arm for Mateo to grab. He swam out and with effort tossed one leg of the trousers to Santiago. Santiago was able to catch the trousers with his fingertips and then with his whole hand. The current was moving him and Mateo down away from me, but I held my ground against the current. I heard a rip as his trousers separated, but not before Santiago was able to catch Mateo's hand. I felt a great sense of relief as we made our way to shore. "I thought I was going to lose you." I said. "Both of you. I couldn't handle losing my friends so quickly." Santiago caught his breath. "Thanks to both of you I'm alive. You're not going to lose friends that easily. We are together." He slung his wet and ripped trousers over his shoulders as we walked naked back to where we had left our clothes. That evening we brought the woman up the beach with some food and whiskey. We built a campfire and took turns with the woman in the brush behind the campfire. Santiago went first while Mateo and I tipped back a shared bottle and some food. By the time Santiago emerged with his trousers around his ankles Mateo was tipsy as he moved through the brush removing his shirt as he went. "Yes. This is the life." Santiago said as he downed the whiskey. "Thanks to you!" We were left listening to the moans coming from the brush and climax. Soon Mateo emerged naked and covering his partially erect member with his hands. "Your turn." He said drunkenly. "I've got her ready for you." He said as he threw himself to the sand. I got up unsteadily to my feet and started pulling my shirt off. I threw the shirt to the ground and walked myself out of my trousers and left them behind as I went through the brush. The woman was lying there naked with her loincloth to one side where Santiago had pulled it off. She had tears in her eyes but I didn't notice that. I wondered then that I had forgotten her name. I knew she had one. I knew that the priests had baptized her so she had a Christian name. I couldn't remember what it was. "Well. I don't know what your name is," I said, holding my rapidly rising cock in one hand, "But tonight I'm calling you 'Joy' because that's what you're bringing us." I entered her with the sounds of my friends laughing a few paces away.

Our needs met we spent the rest of the night drinking on the beach leaving the woman to find her own way back to the ship.

Then Cortez announced his plan and I knew that I would have to take a stand. "Men," he started, "Spanish law allows a group of Spaniards anywhere to set up their own city with the authorization of the king. We have set up our own city and I am the mayor. Here is the paperwork announcing to the world the first Spanish city in this land of the Mexica. Men. I give you the city of Vera Cruz!" He had already performed this legal fiction with his most loyal supporters. I, as the nephew of the governor, was left out of the planning. I suppose he didn't trust me enough to confide his plans in me. I'd like to think that if he had confided in me the future might have been different, but that is the way of life. This new city of Vera Cruz was legal with all the legal seals and documents on paper proclaiming it a city under King Charles V. Cortez had removed himself from the control of my uncle and basically proclaimed himself mayor or governor of this new land. For him it was a brilliant move because if they went back to Cuba now my uncle would have the legal right to take his fifth after sending the King's fifth to Spain. The rest of the treasure could be distributed any way he desired. By making himself a mayor under the king he had control of all the treasure after deducting the King's fifth.

I should have realized that before I protested. "Are you turning your back on the governor? Are you proclaiming yourself governor?" I protested. I, of course, was still listed as bookkeeper for the voyage and thought I had some influence over Cortez. My mind was on the gold that we had obtained already while his was on the gold and land we could obtain. His answer to my protest was to throw me in irons. I should have expected that. I was held in irons while gallows and stocks were built in front of me. He wasn't letting our friendship stand in his way. Cortez said "There will be no going back. I'll let you think about where you want to stand." I was shocked at my sudden loss of trust. Then came the worst blow. "Bring his belongings out from the ship." He commanded. "I shall see of his loyalty." My heart sank as Cortez went through my belongings and found the bracelet and extra book detailing how I had taken more money in than what was reported in the first book. His eyes turned hard and his voice was steely "I trusted you." He whispered to me with hate in his voice. He then proclaimed in front of the whole crew. "I trusted you and called you my friend and this is how you treat me and your fellow crew." My heart sank to hear my deeds exposed to public. I really did consider Cortez my friend and started to protest, "Sir. I am your friend," but was silenced with a hard slap to my face. "No. You are no friend of mine. You are a thief and I shall show you how we deal with thieves," he concluded as he gave me another hard slap to the face. "Strip him and place him in the pillory. Let the others show their contempt to a thief. Take his woman and give her to someone else." I was quickly and roughly removed of my clothing by willing and and angry crew members. Santiago, as chief of security looked at me as he tore the shirt from my body, "I trusted you. We were friends you bastard. Look what you've done." I was placed naked in the newly erected stocks while Cortez tore my second accounting book apart in front of me. My eyes faced the new gallows as I imagined my fate. "You have attempted to cheat His Majesty out of his rightful part of the treasure." He said ripping another page in front of my eyes." You have stolen from me," ripping another page. "You have stolen from the crew," and a hard slap to the face. Then the worst blow of all. "You claimed to be my friend," and a final slap to my face. "By rights you should be put to death." I shivered as my manhood pulled closer to my body. "You shall stay in these stocks as an example to others and let everyone show their contempt to a thief. I shall start with twenty lashes"

I stood there, naked, with my head and arms trapped in the stocks. In that brief moment I saw the collapse of my life. I'd lost the friendship of Santiago and Mateo. Cortez was ready to send me to the gallows and I would be lucky to escape the noose. I thought of Alejandro being tied, helpless to the railing. I didn't have long to think as Cortez himself gave the first twenty lashes as the others counted them off after each scream escaping my lips. It was a stroke of genius on his part. He had successfully set up this new city and pulled himself away from my uncle. The legal framework only lacked the King's signature to make it official. This signature would be had when Cortez sent the gold to Spain. I was sure that the King would sign the document when he saw how rich he could be. I was the object lesson to show others that he was in command and no dissent would be allowed. If I wasn't crying in pain I would have admired his actions.

I was held in the stocks for a couple of days. For two days I was treated with contempt by others. I felt dried horse dung thrown at my back. Others threw stones. More than once I felt the lash of a whip on my naked body. Just as I woke once from the pain in my back I felt a belt rip across my ass. I couldn't see who did it, but I cried in agony till finally whoever was doing it stopped and I heard sniffles as if he were trying to cover up crying. I had a lot of time to think as I drifted in and out of consciousness moaning in pain. In my agony the first night as I came out of consciousness I felt a knife across my neck. "I could do it now you know," came the whispered voice from behind me as the knife made its way between the stocks and my neck. The knife played on my neck for a moment as I tried not to move. "Or perhaps I could cut you down here," came the whispered voice again as the knife moved down my chest and past my naval before finally stopping with the blade against my cock. "Yes. I know about you," continued the voice. "That would hurt more than a flogging." The blade stroked down my penis and finally stopped with a tug against my sac, while I whimpered in terror. "Yes I could do that here, but I'm going to make you suffer. I want you to spend the rest of this expedition worrying when I'm going to kill you, but I will kill you." With a final flick of the knife that shaved the hair above my cock he disappeared in the darkness. I stood there fastened to the stocks still trying to decide through my pain if I had dreamt it or not. Something was familiar about the voice. It sounded like one of the sailors, but in my pain I couldn't think if it was Mateo or Santiago or somebody else from the ship. Pain took over and I drifted back into unconsciousness.

I awoke again, still in pain. My mind was clearer now. I still couldn't place where I had heard the voice before, but it was clear enough to think. Cortez was right. I was trying to steal from the king at least. One could argue that I was stealing from the crew, because I knew that the crew was last in line to get paid. What really hurt was the slap of "you claimed to be my friend." I considered myself the

friend of Cortez and now that friendship was broken.
Finally after two days Cortez stood over me as judge and
executioner. "You have stolen from me, the crew and king.
By law you should be put to death, but we are short handed
and I believe that you can make a strong soldier and am
willing to accept you as part of the new army. Otherwise
your fate would be up to the laws of Vera Cruz. I will let
you think about your response." Cortez had said that I
could think about my response. I had my response right
away. I was the example and warning to the entire crew, or
now city. I knew when I was beat. I had no choice. I
could swing from a rope here on the beach or I could join
Cortez as a soldier. I chose the soldier life. I suppose I
deserved the treatment. I had the two books, which
although common, I hadn't shared with either Cortez or
my uncle. At the end Cortez came and asked my my
choice. "Sir." I said weakly, "I choose to come with you."
At the end of two days of pain I was pulled from the
stocks. I fell to the ground covered in my own excrement,
unable to stand and clutching at my neck that had been
encased in the stocks. Immediately I was pulled from the
stocks and given treatment for my wounds. Cortez was
always magnanimous in victory whether with the natives
or his soldiers. "We shall conquer this land and make a
great colony for the king."

I was allowed to return to the new city of Vera Cruz,
but I had lost any status I had. As a thief I was the lowest
form of life onboard ship even though we were no longer

at sea. As I was pulled away from the pillory I heard muttering of "hanging's too good for him," and "better watch your back." My previous friendship with Cortez had given me some kind of elevated status and now I was nothing. Santiago ordered two sailors to lead/carry me away and I was spat on as I was led away. I felt that I had no friends left among the 600 or so that had started the journey. Some of the native women were called to treat my wounds. Since they did not speak Spanish I don't know how much they knew of what was going on. No matter, they treated me kindly. I assume that they were used to treating the victims of violence. I moaned with pain as they cleaned the blood from my back and legs. I was sunburned from two days in the sun and I cried as the women dressed the wounds and burns with ointment. "It will get better." I heard a voice say. "Let the women treat you. They know what they are doing." I looked up from where I was laying on my stomach to see Fr. Aguilar. "After I escaped from the sacrifice area I was captured as a slave. They treated me worse than that and I was able to survive." He continued. "You will too. You will feel better. I'll go now, but come back to see you soon." Then saying something to the native woman attending me he left. The woman seemed to soften her treatment and continued talking to the other women surrounding me. I slept most of the day and the next. I hung on to Aguilar's words whether or not I thought they were a dream. After the third day I started to feel better and I was able to hobble to the latrine and the onshore mess hall. In both places I was ignored and still heard muttering as I went through the line for food. I ate alone and in silence and went back to the tent that had been set up as a hospital. To my surprise Aguilar was waiting for me. "How do you feel now?" he asked. "Somewhat better, but nobody talks to me." Looking at me he stated the obvious that still surprised me with its truth. "Do you blame them?" I was stunned for a moment and then forced to consider my life. "I guess you're right. I deserved what I got. I planned the two books from the start, but I always wanted to be a friend of Cortez." I added. Aguilar looked at me as only a priest could, "Did you? Or were you using him to further your own goals?" I was hit hard in the face with this realization. Every meeting I had had with him was all part of a plan to get on this expedition. It had started on the ship from Spain when the sailors told me that if I wanted to go on an expedition I should meet Cortez. I had carefully arranged everything from buying beer to boisterous visits to the whore house. Of course the biggest part of my plan was made when my uncle suggested that I try to make acquaintance with Cortez, little knowing that I had fostered that relationship for months. "You see Esteban," continued Aguilar, "we all have the selfish part inside that refuses to help others. It's fine to care for yourself, but have you put yourself before anybody else in your life? Do high spirits get in the way of service?" I gasped in shock as the priest used my mother's words to convict me. I thought about everything I had done up till now and knew I needed to make amends. "Father forgive me," I began, using the phrase I hadn't used for a long time. "It has been two years since my last confession."

Fr. Aguilar became my mentor as I tried to rebuild my life as a common soldier. The priest who had gone through his own hell for years and was trying to rebuild his own life became a willing intermediary between me and God as well as a harder audience: my fellow soldiers. "You have been granted absolution by the Church and God," he said, "but now you have to work with your fellow man. They will be more difficult. I can go before you to ease the way, but you are going to have to do the hard work and hope they believe you." He made a few discrete connections among the crew and I went one on one to apologize and ask forgiveness starting with the sailors who had been the loudest when I was pulled from the stocks. To my surprise the loudest sailor was the quickest to forgive me. Fr. Aguilar brought me to him and introduced us "Diego this is Esteban and he would like to talk to you for a few minutes. I'll leave now so you two can talk." I gulped as I faced my fears and past. "Yes. I just wanted to apologize to you and others for stealing from you. I was wrong and I hope that you'll forgive me. If you don't I suppose I deserve that too." Diego looked at me for a moment as if he was thinking about what to say. "Well I'm glad you admitted your mistakes." He said. "Some people would just try to go on." When I said that Fr. Aguilar had seen through my excuses right away he replied, "Yes he can do that." Then pausing as if he didn't want to go further, "When he came to me and said that you would like to talk with me I at first refused and said that Cortez should have killed you. I was angry and told him I thought you got off easy. Fr. Aguilar asked me about my life and we talked for a long time." Finally after another pause he lifted his shirt to reveal his back covered with the scars of the whip. "You see. I was really just as bad as you and I didn't want to face my own faults."

It was soon after this that fate smiled on Cortez again. I was still healing from my treatment and a group of natives came up the shore. The translating duo of Malinche and Aguilar met with them and Cortez and we received an invitation to visit who we now know as the Toltanacs. Cortez invited me to come with the small group to visit the Toltec town. I say I was invited, but I think I was commanded as Cortez did not entirely trust me yet.

We took the day to walk and ride up the beach to meet the Toltanacs. Malinche and Aguilar came as well as Bernal and a few of Cortez' trusted men. The rest were left in Vera Cruz to keep with orders that anyone who tried to rise in support of my uncle would be quickly put down. I felt that they didn't need to worry. The stocks and gallows that served as a reminder of my treason were still there.

We arrived and met with the local chief who complained about the Mexica and the fact that the Toltanacs had to pay a tribute to the Mexica chief

Montezuma as well as a steady supply of children for sacrifice. When I heard that my heart ached. What kind of people were these to sacrifice children? True I had been held in the stocks for two days and bore the scars on my back of being whipped but I knew deep down that I had deserved this punishment. I was now eighteen years old and a man. These were children being consigned to death on a sacrificial stone and didn't deserve it. The Toltanacs wanted help from Cortez and Cortez needed an ally if he wished to gain control of the Mexica. Cortez ordered our move from the new town of Vera Cruz to the land of the Toltanacs.

Since the Toltanacs were eager to have us in their territory we set about building a real city instead of just an encampment with stocks and gallows. We worked hard at building houses, a market and church: everything a Spanish town would need.

Tenochtitlan
Cuauhtémoc Speaks

Montezuma is sure that this man is Quetzalcoatl returned from the East and is afraid to confront him and destroy our civilization. He is still hoping that he will tire of waiting at the coast and move on. He briefly held hope when the runners reported that the group had left their camp, but that hope was dashed when other runners reported that he had moved to the land of the Toltanacs. "I have ordered my tax collectors to tell the Toltanacs to quit helping the white men. As punishment for receiving them they must supply us with twenty for sacrifice." I felt briefly happy that Montezuma was taking a hard line against the invader. If we could force the Toltanacs to quit supporting the invaders they might leave of hunger. I was happy only till I realized that a jaguar is most dangerous when he is cornered.

Vera Cruz
Esteban Speaks

Our new city of Vera Cruz was looking very nice and I was starting to feel comfortable even though it was hot and humid by the shore. One day several Mexica arrived in the city and the local leaders went in to a turmoil. Cortez was summoned by the chief, "Montezuma is angry that we have aided you and demands that we stop and also requires twenty children for sacrifice," he concluded with tears in his eyes. Cortez listened carefully and I could see that he was developing a plan in his mind. Although we had started as adversaries I was now seeing how his mind worked and he always had a plan. "Arrest them," he told the chief. "If anything happens my army will protect you." The chief was worried but finally agreed to arrest the tax collectors and they were thrown in the Toltanac equivalent of a jail. That evening I was sent with Santiago, Aguilar and Malinche under cover of darkness and we were told to release the tax collectors. I felt comfortable with Aguilar. He had helped me at the lowest time in my life. I tried to talk with Santiago, but he responded with "Damn it. You've ruined everything. Cortez trusted me and now he can't trust me because of you." I apologized again and walked ahead to be with Aguilar and Malinche. They were speaking in that native language she used that sounded like birds singing. "She says that you will have to work hard to regain trust but it can happen." Said Aguilar. "But first you have to change yourself." That was easier said than done I thought. I wondered how much she had had to change. She had been born to one family and then sold or traded to another village. I didn't understand the relationships and how they worked here in this new world. Malinche spoke the two languages and was using that to her advantage. True she was still a concubine for one of Cortez' lieutenants, but it could have been worse for her. She could have been like the woman I had had for those few days who now was being passed among various men even though she was the daughter of a village chief. As the lowest soldier in the army I would never have a chance at her again. As we got closer to the village where the tax collectors were jailed Santiago called for us. "We are to release the tax collectors without the Toltanacs knowing and bring them to Cortez. You!" He said," pointing at me. "Go ahead of us and search the area surrounding the central square where we were today. The tax collectors should be in a cage or cell somewhere near there. Find them and report back to me." I had an idea that he was sending me alone so that if captured by the Toltonacs I would be no great loss to the expedition and probably earn what I deserved on the sacrificial stone instead of the gallows. The fact that he hadn't used my name told me that I had a long way to go to earn his trust. I was determined to at least earn Santiago's trust even if I couldn't earn friendship again. I silently worked my way through the village in search of anything that could be a jail. Fortunately the city was empty. I guess the city fathers didn't think they needed guards to hold the universally hated tax collectors. Finally some paces off the center square I came upon a large hole in the ground with a wooden lattice work frame covering if. The frame was held in place by heavy rocks and thick rope. It would have been nearly impossible for the prisoners to release themselves from the inside. I was fairly certain that I had discovered the prison, but carefully checked the area before I approached. Seeing no guards under nearby trees or houses I went forward and checked the hole. The tax collectors were there looking up at me in the moonlight. I quickly returned to Santiago and reported where they were. I led the three of us to the pit and Malinche told them in their own language to be quiet and they would be released. Aguilar and I untied the rope and moved one rock so it would look like it had been pushed away from the inside. Soon the four men joined us as we returned to the ship and brought them to Cortez. "I have rescued you from the

Toltanacs and I am releasing you to go back to Montezuma. But you are to tell him this that I am coming to visit him as a friend and to bring greetings from the great king Charles V." Malinche then told them to leave before dawn so they could be well on their way before the sun rose. I was impressed by what Cortez had done. He had planned everything so he could appear as a great man to Montezuma.

Tenochtitlan
Cuauhtémoc Speaks

The white men are on their way. My cousin is beside himself with worry. "The tax collectors that I sent to intimidate the Toltanacs were jailed and then rescued by this man who calls himself Cortez. He sent them back with a message that he had rescued them and now plans on visiting here." I had no advice to give my cousin. He is sure that this Cortez is Quetzalcoatl returned. I returned to my house sure that Cortez was somehow behind the arrest of the tax collectors.

Vera Cruz
Esteban Speaks

We are preparing to depart our new city for Tenochtitlan as Cortez told the tax collectors when he freed them. He also promised the Toltanacs that he would protect them if Montezuma attacked. But first we were to discover the dark side of our new friendship. The Toltanacs had been very gracious and kind to us. We were kept supplied with food and the chiefs had presented more women to Cortez. They were meant as wives to the elite of our new city. I was, of course, not considered an elite anymore so my desires had to be satisfied with any local girl willing to be with me. It was after this presentation that we discovered the dark side of the culture. No sooner had the women been presented than five naked young men were pulled from the recently used tax collector cell. At first I wondered why these prisoners were being brought to us. I thought maybe they were another gift to Cortez as slaves or servants. Immediately the first young man who looked no older than I was pulled away from the others and grabbed by four men with one at each limb. The man who had looked resigned to slavery when he first came from the cell now started screaming. The four men held him fast as a priest in a brightly colored flowered cape and loin cloth swung a knife high above his head and then dove it deep into the man's chest and pulled out his still beating heart and threw it into a fire. The blood was then sprinkled around the crowd almost like a priest would sprinkle holy water. I felt sick to my stomach. Although Fr. Aguilar had told us what he had witnessed and escaped from I was not prepared for what I saw. It continued as four other young men were paraded in front of us and each took their turn on the sacrificial stone. I could hold it no longer. I ran from the city and vomited. On my knees with vomit dripping from my mouth I cried, and although I don't pray often, I asked God what I was doing there.

Cortez was incensed. "Your sacrifices are terrible. You need to quit now." He demanded of the chief. The chief was just as angry. "We cannot quit the sacrifice! The god would be angry and we would have no crops." Cortez tried assuring him that the crops would not fail. He finally convinced the chief to allow a chapel to the virgin in place of one of the gods. The men wasted no time in pulling down one of the gods and placing a portrait of Our Lady in its place. The chief was angry but Cortez assured him that Our Lady would protect him and the city. "If anything happens I will be here to protect you." He said.

Cortez then continued his process to make our city a legal city in the sight of the King. He prepared all the documents with seals and notaries. He separated out more than the King's Fifth of gold along with the banner of Quetzalcoatl that had been given to them. He put everything on one of the smaller ships and told the captain to go directly to Spain and report to the King what had been done in his name. He gave names of friends in the Royal Court and said, "Talk to them. Show them the documents, but give them to nobody but the king himself. Wait for his answer that we are a new city and I am the governor."

The ship left and I felt alone again. The crew saw one of the ships leave and some felt stranded again and talked about going back to Cuba. I talked with Diego and together we talked with the crew, "I say we have to trust Cortez. Look at what he has accomplished so far. I think we can trust him to get us the rest of the way." The other men didn't look too impressed with my speech but then Cortez then came forward and gave another rousing speech about the gold we would gain if we went forward to Tenochtitlan. He reminded us about duty to King and the Cross. "We have life if we go backward. We go forward for gold. We go forward for Spain. We go forward for Charles." He concluded to cheers from the crew. He then ordered the remaining ships to be driven ashore and burnt. I stood in shock as I watched the burning ships We were now truly stranded in this new world. We had no choice now but to follow Cortez to the end of the world or to death.

Journey to Tenochtitlan

Tenochtitlan
Cuauhtémoc Speaks

The white men are on their way. Montezuma has not ordered the vassal towns along the route to fight them. My runners tell me that Montezuma's runners have told them nothing. If the vassal towns realize that these invaders are a threat to them as well as us perhaps we have a chance. The people here know little yet about this invader, but if this Cortez continues without being stopped word will get out on the street. Perhaps people will stay in the valley; perhaps they will leave to safer areas.

Vera Cruz
Esteban Speaks

We are leaving. I am scared and nervous, but ready to leave the hot and humid coast. Cortez sent a letter to the King with the ship that left with the request for city charter describing his plans. He has since written letters to the King that will eventually be received describing our successes and payments of gold. Since Cortez spared my life back at Vera Cruz I am, for now, fully supportive of his plan. To do any less is to invite the lash, or worse, the gallows. I took a last look at the burnt out remnants of the ships and felt stranded here but knowing I had no other choice but forward made me feel stronger.

On the 15ᵗʰ of August, the year of our Lord 1519 we left Vera Cruz with 400 soldiers. The Toltonocs provided men as porters to move cannon and luggage. The women brought up the rear except for Malinche who stayed close to Aguilar to provide translation. Cortez had left the older soldiers back at Vera Cruz to guard the city and help the Toltonocs if needed. We started out through the Toltonoc territory and for more than a week we slowly continued higher in the mountains leaving the hot and humid coast behind.

Since I had lost any type of status in the community I spent most of my time with Diego and Fr. Aguilar. "It's getting cooler," I said. "I wonder how cold it will get. I haven't been this cold since I left Spain." Aguilar nodded. "Yes it's getting colder and yes it will be colder still. When I was first captured I was brought this high to be sacrificed." I had forgotten that he had nearly been sacrificed. "Tell us again how it was." Diego said. "It was terrible. We could see everything that happened to everybody. I was just lucky that one night the guards didn't lock the cage well and Guerrero and I were able to escape. Maybe those guards took our place on the sacrificial stone the next day." Aguilar looked at Diego. "Tell us Diego. What is your story?" His story was the opposite of mine. "I come from Madrid, the result of a drunken night between two angry people. My mother married my father when she found out she was pregnant, but there was never any love between the two." I nodded. If I had to say one thing about my parents they were devoted to each other. I was the one who had caused them the most problems. Diego continued "When I was young my mother died and my brothers and I were left alone with a father who was usually lost in the bottle. By the time I was 10 I was living on the streets and by the time I was 13 I had signed myself up on one of Colon's later voyages." I silently compared our two lives. Mine of abundance and his of poverty and how both of us now were on equal standing. "I've been at sea for fifteen years and I suppose I'll die at sea." Since it was just the three of us I asked, "When we first started talking down at the beach you showed me your back and said we were the same. How did you get those scars? Will you tell us?" Diego paused for a moment as if he were angry and then smiled. "Yes. I suppose I should. I shouted at you that hanging was too good for you. I really should have been shouting at me. Some time ago when I was about your age we were on the stretch from Spain to the new world and we knew we should be getting closer to land but kept seeing nothing. Our rations were getting low and so the captain put us on limited rations. We basically missed one meal a day so we could stretch our rations. I was young and impulsive and hungry. One night when everyone had gone to sleep I roamed the ship till I got to the storeroom and broke in to find some crackers. I was eating them when I was caught by the quartermaster. He made enough noise to wake up half the ship and I was tied up and thrown in the brig until the captain had time to deal with me. The next morning while I was in the brig I heard the shout of "Land ho" and I thought I would soon be released since we would have food and water." I interrupted, "Did they release you?" "Of course not," came the quick reply. "I had stolen food and according to the captain it didn't matter if I had done it right before landing. The captain had me stretched out on a grate in front of the whole crew to receive two dozen lashes." I frowned at the thought. "So we are alike." I said. "No. I was angry because I was caught the day before we hit land and in my mind it wasn't right. I carried that anger until you came to apologize to me. When I saw you being released from the pillory I still refused to see that I had done anything wrong. It wasn't until you," he said, looking at Fr. Aguilar, "asked me if why I was so angry that I realized I wasn't angry at you, but angry at myself." Fr. Aguilar smiled, "We often project our worst faults on to another person. I think you've both learned a lot." Diego laughed, "thanks to you it only took Esteban a few days to learn, while it took me about 10 years."

After ten days of travel we left Toltonoc territory and entered Xocotla. Our porters told us that this was a town that belonged to Montezuma and didn't know what kind of reception to expect. We got a poor reception until the porters told the others about our weapons and the gifts that

Montezuma had already given. Here they told the Xolotlans that Montezuma considered Cortez a god. Cortez only said that he was coming as a representative of the great King Charles V in friendship to see Montezuma. When the Xocotlans heard about our weapons and that Cortez was considered a god they became much more friendly. They gave us food and supplies and even some warm clothes. I was starting to remember fondly the heat and humidity of the coast.

The food was better and warm clothing appreciated and then good news came. The Xolotlans told Cortez that once he left their territory they would be in the land of Tlaxcala. The Tlaxcalans were enemies of Montezuma and they might be considered friendly to Cortez. The entire Spaniard party was happy at the news and Cortez ordered several of the Toltonacs to go ahead to tell the Tlaxcalans that Cortez was coming in peace and wanted to ally himself against Montezuma. The envoys were given gifts and were sent on their way. The rest of us enjoyed some time of peace and relaxation while waiting for the return of the envoy and hopefully good news of an alliance.

While we waited for news from Tlaxcala I tried again to talk with Santiago and Mateo. I decided that it would be better to talk to them individually. Mateo wasn't involved in ship security and discipline so he might be more open to talk. He saw me coming and tried to move, but I was too fast for him. "I just want to talk," I said, "and apologize for what I did and breaking our friendship. I know I don't deserve your friendship now, but I'd like to try." Mateo stared at me for a moment and looked like he wanted to walk away again. "It will never be the same again. We are under suspicion. Some of the officers think that we were a part of your deal since we all shared the cabin and all our work stuff was on the same desk in the cabin." I paled at the thought that I had destroyed other lives besides my own. "I think it best that we not be seen together. You deserved the lash, but I don't want to receive a whipping because of what other people think. I'm sorry, but that's they way it has to be." I left, crestfallen that my actions had wrecked Santiago and Mateo's lives too. Later I told Diego everything, "I didn't mean to put them under suspicion. I didn't mean to lose their friendship. I just want..." I started, but Diego finished for me, "You just wanted money. Admit it. You wanted money more than you wanted friends." I had to admit that he was right. "So what do I do?" I asked. "You have to go on. Maybe you'll never be friends with them again, but maybe you'll make new friends and improve your life."

Nobody came from Tlaxcala and murmurs turned in to grumbling. After several days Cortez ordered us to continue on the route to Tlaxcala with or without permission. On the road we discovered the envoys coming back to us. "Sir. They don't believe that you are coming in peace. They believe it is a trick of Montezuma to get them to relax so he can send in his armies. They took the four of us and caged us with other captives for sacrifice. The last thing they said to us was that they had an army of 60,000 ready to fight you. We were caged for two nights before we were able to escape and return to you." Cortez rewarded the men for their courage and publicly thanked them for their bravery. "We will continue on to give glory to God and the Virgin. We will continue for our King."

We continued until one of the Xolotlans said that we had now entered Tlaxcalan territory and returned home. We had been on the road two weeks. I felt very alone and very afraid. That fear turned to terror within a few hours as we were attacked from the side. Cortez ordered us to form battle lines around the supplies and the battle commenced. We had cannon and rifles so we had some advantage but they seemed fearless in their attacks. I had my sword that I now used without fear. The memory of the young man sprawled out on the sacrificial stone with his still beating heart being held up to the sun spurred me to attack without fear. I did not want to be one of the sacrifices. Diego and I fought side by side with sword in what seemed a never ending parade of Tlaxcalans ready to attack us.

I don't know how we managed it but we fought till sunset and the army disappeared in the woods. Cortez said he estimated the army at 6,000 men, much less than what the Tlaxcalans were said to have. I settled down for the night happy in the believe that the worst was over. That was not to be. The next day the army was back with even more men.This went on for a week and every day we lost more men and horses. Some men were ready to go back to

Vera Cruz and wait for reinforcements. They said that we could go back because eventually the king would send help after hearing nothing about his new colony. Or, they said. "Velazquez will send a party out looking for us." Cortez at first showered us with praise for what we had done so far. "You have beaten an army far outnumbering you. If we leave now we break face with those we have befriended. The Toltonocs and Xolota will refuse to have us near them for fear of Montezuma." He concluded with "It is forward or death. Forward for the glory of King Charles and Forward to spread the Gospel of Christ and the Blessed Virgin." He didn't say that if we retreated we would probably face death by sacrifice. He didn't say, but the men still remembered the dead body being thrown from the sacrificial stone.

The battles continued and we lost more men until finally on September 20 a Tlaxcalan general came from the woods. "We ask for peace now. We thought that you were from Montezuma. We did not know who you were." When he said that I wondered if he thought Cortez was a god. Some of the natives seemed to think that and the Toltonocs had implied that to the Xolotans. Maybe we were now better off because of that. "We were sure that Montezuma had arranged for you to attack us and we could not allow that. Please come to the city of Tlaxcala now. The entire city waits to welcome you and celebrate an alliance against Montezuma." Cortez wasn't going to let him off too easily and reminded him that the envoys had specifically said who they were and the general was forced to repeat that the city waited and they wanted an alliance.

We moved a day's march away to the city of Tlaxcala and were treated as great friends. It was at this time that envoys from Montezuma arrived. They were brought before Cortez who received them as great friends. "I desire to come and visit my dear friend and my king's dear brother," he said to the visible consternation of the envoys. "When I finish here with my friends the Tlaxcalans." He concluded with special emphasis. The envoys smiled and gave Cortez gifts and the offer of more gold if he would leave. Cortez again said how his greatest desire was to come and visit "my good friend" in Tenochtitlan.

Tenochtitlan
Cuauhtémoc Speaks

Disaster. Cortez is on his way. He has defeated Tlaxcala. My runners tell me that Tlaxcala fought well but were overpowered by sticks that kill and magic swords that destroy buildings and trees at great distance. Cortez was immune to the magic forces that the Tlaxcalan priests sent against him. They set out magic threads and Cortez went right through them. He also ignored the magic pictures that should have repelled them. Montezuma is sure that he is Quetzalcoatl returned and sent his nephews as envoys with gifts and offers of gold if he would just turn around. Cortez refused and said how much he looked forward to visiting

Montezuma in Tenochtitlan. Montezuma seems at a loss of what to do. He dare not kill a god, but dare not let him come and take the throne. Word has now gotten out to the people and they are worried. That is all that people talk about in the market. Some people have left the city to seek safety in the country.

Tlaxcala
Esteban Speaks

Tlazcala is a very pleasant city with ordered streets and beautiful marketplaces. The people were very friendly and the leaders had given more women to Cortez and his lieutenants. These women were properly Baptized and given to the men.   Were it not for temples with skulls of sacrificial victims I would have felt right at home.

I saw that some of the new women had been spread around more officers. I, of course, was no longer living with Mateo or Santiago. I was now a lowly soldier sleeping where I could and preparing my own food where and when I could. I saw one of the women go to the tent that Mateo and Santiago now shared and an arm reached out of the tent to pull her in. It appeared that one or both of of my former friends had convinced Cortez of their innocence enough to allow them a women of their own to cook, clean, and provide comfort. I thought no more of it. I had lost that privilege and I doubted I would get it back again.

Instead I tried to made amends with others near me. I found that despite there being 600 men who left Vera Cruz there were only two people who were known by everybody: Cortez and myself. Cortez the great leader who had led us against countless odds this far and Velazquez the thief who kept two books and stole gold from the treasure. I used Aguilar as my intermediary again to talk with the group of soldiers I was now assigned to. He waited till they were all gathered around the fire one night before we sought shelter wherever we could. "I'd like you to take a few moments and listen to what Esteban has to say." One soldier said. "That thief! If we fight again I'll make sure he is captured. He'll make a good sacrifice!" Aguilar paused for a moment long enough for the soldiers to think. "Take a few moments and listen and as far as the sacrifice I escaped from sacrifice. It's not something I want any of you to go through." I thanked Aguilar and stood before the group. I think I felt about the same as when I stood naked in the pillory. "I wanted to come here today and apologize for what I did. I really have no excuse. Like Cortez said I deserved death but he gave me a chance." I paused again, "When I was young a friend and I took money from the alms plate at the church and we never got caught. Maybe if I had gotten caught I would have been a different person but I don't know. I know that I cheated you here and got caught and punished. I'll show you the scars on my back if you want. I would like the chance to earn your trust as a fellow soldier. I suppose it's too much to ask to earn your respect or even your friendship, but I hope to earn your trust that when it comes to battle I will fight with you and not against you." I sat down. Nobody said anything for a moment until finally a man I only knew as Tomas said "I imagine that we've all done things we're not proud of. I saw you in the pillory and I'll admit I took a belt to your ass out of pure anger. I think it was more fear at our predicament than anger at you. If you're man enough to come and talk to all of us I'm willing to trust you as a soldier. And friend." He extended his hand and I shook it grateful for the chance at redemption. A few men walked away, but several more came forward and shook my hand, "I'll give you a chance," and, "proud to serve with you." Said two men I later identified as Gabriel and Martin. "Thank you," I said to those who had stayed. "I promise to do my best to earn your trust and, if I can, your friendship." I went to bed that night with several new friends and a new found respect for Aguilar.

Cortez wanted to end human sacrifice here as he had at the shore but was persuaded out of it. He knew that although the Tlaxcalans had allied themselves with him his position was too tenuous to roll a god down the temple as he had with the Toltonocs. He spent some time talking with the leaders of the Tlaxcala and pumped them for information about Tenochtitlan. They told him how it was a city built on an island and the story surrounding the flight from the north. "It is a large city with many bridges. If you try to take it they will just pull up the bridges and be alone on the island. You will not be able to take it." They even described how deep the water was in the lake. The Tlazcalans wanted to take advantage of their new found alliance and go with Cortez as part of a conquering army. Cortez said no. "I am only visiting Montezuma as a representative of my king." He told the Tlaxcalans repeatedly. I'm sure that all the men knew otherwise, but this was the same thing he told every native leader who asked.

Finally the envoys from Montezuma returned and asked what Cortez wished to do. "I wish to see my good friend Montezuma and give greetings from his brother emperor my king, King Charles V." They looked nervous but suggested that Cortez move us to Cholula which was closer to Tenochtitlan. The Tlaxcalans were worried. "Cholula is not part of the Tlaxcala confederation." We were told. "It is free, but under the control of Montezuma. You won't be safe there." Cortez listened carefully, but decided to go ahead. The Tlaxcalans wanted to send their whole army with him but he declined. "I don't want to appear as a conquering army. I only wish to visit Montezuma." He finally consented to 6000 soldiers to come with him but asked them to stay outside the city.

We had now been on the way for several weeks, and I was still somewhat isolated from the others. Before the flogging I had spent most of my time with Santiago and Mateo and sometimes Cortez. Now I was estranged from them, but only loosely connected to my new comrades, the soldiers. Since we had started out with eleven ships and some 600 men I didn't know everybody. In fact until we left Vera Cruz for Tenochtitlan there had always been a good number of men remaining on the ships so we had never been all together at once. Of course, once Cortez sent a ship to Spain with its crew and burnt the other ships we were now all together.

We marched our way to Cholula which took a couple days with all our equipment. Once there the Tlaxcalan army kept their word and stayed outside the city. This worried the Cholulans who asked the Mexica to send an army too. Soon the area seemed like an army camp with soldiers everywhere except in the city. Rumors started to fly. I couldn't understand where the rumors were coming from. Some were sure that Tlaxcala would attack. Others that the Mexica army would attack. Cortes heard rumors from Malinche and others and finally decided to take action.

The battle for Cholula had been carefully planned by Cortez to impress Montezuma and control a key city. The leaders of the city were invited to a banquet at the city hall where they were to be arrested. We were to run through the courtyard killing everybody we could while the leaders were locked in the dining hall. At his signal we started through the courtyard, Diego and Martin by my side. I remembered the knife fighting techniques that Felipe had taught me as we worked our way through the courtyard.

114

Our assignment was to fight our way through the courtyard, and then make it to the city gate to open for the Tlaxcalans. We slashed our way through the courtyard and made it to the entrance. Diego opened the gate while I pushed through, "We will hold the gate to keep everyone inside while you run for the city gates." I nodded and shouted as I started out, "I'll be back in a few minutes." The city gates were only a few minutes away and once I got there it was easy enough to push open the gate and run down the trail to where the Tlaxcalans had set up their encampment. Their commanders were waiting for me and soon I found myself left behind as 6000 Tlaxcalans poured toward the loosely guarded gate.

With the shouts of battle in front of me and the silence of the now vacated camp behind me I reveled in the silence. I heard a twig break behind me and started to jump and turn around, but not before a noose settled around my shoulders and I felt a kick to my back that tightened the noose around my arms pinning them to my sides. With one jerk I was pulled backwards falling to the ground and there standing above me was Alejandro. "Maybe I'll do it now," he said, and in a flash I remembered the voice at the pillory. "You! It was you!" I said. "Alejandro, why are you angry at me? I tried to stand up for you! I tried to take your punishment. You saw me being bound and gagged for speaking up!" He stomped a heavy boot on my chest, knocking the wind out of me and spat in my face. "Yes. Sure you tried. You tricked me in to stealing for you and

115

then only when I was strung up for flogging did you say something. You rich bastards think you can do anything and then throw us to the ground." I tried to see through the light of the moon to his face. It was twisted in anger and hate, looking nothing like the Alejandro from the ship. "You let me be flogged and then left the ship to spend the day at the whore house." He spat again and jerked the rope tighter. My arms were pinned, but my legs were free and I attempted to break free by rolling and kicking at Alejandro's legs. My kick missed and the momentum of the kick rolled me and gave Alejandro a chance to deliver a vicious kick to my balls. I moaned in pain and instinctively pulled my knees to my chest. That was all the time Alejandro needed to whip the other end of the rope around my ankles and tie it fast. "Yes," he said as he kicked me in the side and pulled at the noose around my arms. "You spent the day at the whore house like nothing happened and then went on to your rich uncle's house. What did you do there? Gloat at how you tricked the sailor and had him flogged? Yes. Don't look surprised. I heard all about it." I tried to protest again, "No Alejandro. I tried to stop the captain. We were confined to the cabin for a week not allowed to move from the bunk." Another kick to my balls, "Liar. You went from your uncle's house out to your plantation. I suppose you had a big party there too." I tried shouting, "Alejandro listen to me. You knew I was going to the plantation and I wasn't happy. Of course I went to the whore house. I wanted escape from having been confined to the bunk for a week and seeing you being flogged. I got blind drunk but still couldn't forget you being whipped. That's stayed with me to this day." Alejandro looked as if he didn't even hear me. "Yes. I was given three days to recover and then sent back to work. The captain said that I should learn my lesson and be a better worker." He continued in almost a trance. "I showed him. I waited till we docked and let him think everything was good. I worked hard for two days while we were in port and then early the morning of the third day I stole a knife from the tool locker. This knife," waving it in my face, "I slipped in to his cabin and killed him. Those guards never saw me. I slipped over the side and off to the country." I tried struggling out of the rope, but Alejandro had cinched it so tight around my arms that I was losing circulation. Alejandro continued in his trance, "I searched for you and asked around the brothels of town where you were. I made it out to your plantation and thought about killing you then, but you were always with somebody so I returned to town living by thievery. It was then that I got lucky. I heard you and Cortez in the brothel talking about the expedition. I knew I could get onboard one of the ships as a sailor and so I started planning. I couldn't try to come on as a sailor there. I would be recognized quickly. I knew my best chances to get on without being recognized was in Havana so I set off by foot for Havana and waited for you to come. I knew I would have my chance to kill you at some point. I just had to wait." He was in a trance, speaking to me, yet to nobody. I was struggling, but it did no good, every move seemed to make the bonds tighter. "I was so lucky. You were busy everyday in Havana like a dog at Cortez' side. I was able to sign on one of the ships knowing that eventually I would find you alone. I thought I would be able to kill you onboard ship, but you were on another ship. I wasn't able to go to shore till we arrived in Vera Cruz. I saw you go off with Mateo and Santiago and followed you up the beach. I watched you fuck the girl and thought about killing you then, but the others were too close. I knew my time would come." I watched his increasingly erratic behavior and was sure my time had come. "Then I was lucky again. Cortez discovered who you really were and threw you in the pillory. I couldn't flog you like I wanted and the other man whipped your ass, but I enjoyed running my knife over your body and watching you whimper. Oh yes I would have had fun making a eunuch out of you." I squirmed again knowing that I could do nothing against this madman. I started mentally saying the prayers that I should have said much earlier. I was about to become another statistic in the conquest of Tenochtitlan. "Esteban! Esteban! Are you here?" came a shout from the distance. "Fuck," whispered Alejandro. "They're coming. I'll kill you now." And lifted the knife above his head. "Esteban," came the voice again, this time just a few paces away. My eyes were closed expecting the blade to fall, but nothing happened. "Esteban," shouted Martin. "What happened?" In the distance I heard the sound of running footsteps as Alejandro escaped.

"How has he hidden himself all this time?" asked Martin after I had explained the whole thing. Diego added, "we have to tell Cortez. I've never seen this man before, but there were eleven ships and we've only been all together a few weeks. It would have been easy to blend in. He can't get away now. Cortez will order him flogged again." Martin concluded,"it's a good thing we were worried about you and decided to go searching."

"I doubt we will see him again," said Cortez when we finally got back to the city and were able to see him after the fighting and the city was firmly in Spanish hands. "If he has run away he knows he's dead if he comes back here. He has probably fled to Tlaxcala in an attempt to get back to Vera Cruz and another ship to Spain. Describe him to the captains and maybe they know which name he signed on as, but he will probably end up as a slave to the Tlaxcalans and a sacrifice."

Tenochtitlan
Cuauhtémoc Speaks

Cholula is lost. The invader came there under a peace agreement and later looted the city and killed 3000. Cholula believes that he is either Quetzalcoatl returned or another god. He continually talks about a new religion and has even desecrated one of our temples and set a picture of

119

a woman in it. All Montezuma has tried to do to discourage them from coming has failed. Montezuma has sent another delegation apologizing to Cortez for the behavior of the Cholulans, along with more gifts. Now he has invited Cortez to the city. People are fleeing the city. They will assuredly come here next. Is this the end of the world as we know it?

Cholula

Esteban Speaks

We set out from Cholula on a march to Tenochtitlan and Montezuma. The soldiers were in high excitement as we left. True, we were alone again, having left the Tlaxcalan army behind and sent on their way home to Tlaxcala. Cortez wanted to appear in Tenochtitlan as he said, an envoy of the great King Charles V, Holy Roman Emperor. I was still a foot soldier, trusted little more than to carry a sword, with no access to the books or accounting. If we got any more gold I would be in line with the rest of the sailors and soldiers to get money after the King's fifth, Cortez' cut and cost of running the expedition. I'm fairly certain that Cortez forgot that I was an investor in the expedition, although if he had looked closely in the second book he would see that I had already paid myself. I was glad for once that he had torn up the book in front of my face while I stood naked at the pillory.

We left for Tenochtitlan on November 1 and immediately started to climb the mountains. From below it looked like we would have to go between two volcanoes: one of them smoking. We were told that these volcanoes were called Popocatapetl and Iztacciuatl. Melinche translated this as Mountain that Smokes and White Woman. Mountain that Smokes was indeed smoking so it was easy to remember that name. I was also a little worried that it might explode as we got near it. After two days of climbing through the bitter cold and living in fear that the mountain would explode we finally came to the top of the valley between the two mountains. Below stretched out our goal. In the distance we could see the lake of the Mexican valley with an island and various cities around the lake. Of course from this distance we couldn't see anything specific, but we knew we were getting closer to our goal.

Cortez had left the Tlaxcalan army behind because he wanted to appear only as an envoy. Nevertheless, he took seriously our security and ordered everyone to be on alert. It was then on the third day that a group came claiming to be from Montezuma seeking a visit with Cortez. One of the advance guards came and reported "We were doing our reconnaissance and saw this group coming up the trail ahead of us. They were all walking together and, although we couldn't understand them, they seemed like friends. We returned to warn the advance guard and to see what would happen." At this point Aguilar continued the story. "They were brought to Doña Malinche and I so we could see what they wanted. By the time they got to us one of them was being carried on a liter wearing extravagant clothing. He was presented to us as Montezuma." At this point the original guard spoke up, "We were sure that he couldn't be Montezuma because we had seen him walking and talking with the others only a few minutes earlier so we told the advance guard what we had seen. We do not believe he is Montezuma." Cortez smiled briefly. "He must be trying to keep us away again. Thank them for coming but we will not see Montezuma until we arrive in Tenochtitlan."

And so it continued as we went downhill closer to the city on the lake. We passed through various cities and in each city we were greeted warmly and given food and lodging. I was starting to believe that this conquest might be over before it even started till Cortez said "We must be careful to place guards around. This might be a trick to lull us into a sense of security before we are attacked."

It was two days later that another envoy came from Montezuma. Malinche and Aguilar greeted him and brought him before Cortez. "His Majesty is most concerned that you not be troubled about coming to the city." He started, "He is willing to offer you four carts of gold if you do not come any further." Cortez thanked them and again said that he must come to give his greetings from King Charles, "I am commanded to come and explain why I am here. If His Majesty wishes me to leave after that I would be more than happy to go." I felt sure that this last part was not entirely the truth. We wouldn't leave unless we had some gold to show for our work.

Tenochtitlan
Cuauhtémoc Speaks

My cousin has tried everything he can think of. He sent one magical envoy with a man dressed to look like him. If Cortez accepted the magical envoy he would have been unable to recognize the true Montezuma when he came before him. Unfortunately the god that Cortez is saw through the magic and refused to meet with Montezuma's double. The magical envoy came back and Montezuma was forced to send a second group. This group was on their way when they were met in the street by the magic of Smoking Mirror God. The god was dressed as a regular man with long hair and disheveled clothing, but all knew he was Smoking Mirror. Smoking Mirror said that Montezuma had no brains and that Mexico was lost. He announced that through Montezuma's sins Mexico will die. The envoys were so distressed at what Smoking Mirror said that they immediately returned to the palace to report to the king. I was there when they returned and told the king with fear in their voices. They knew that those who delivered bad news could be sacrificed to Huitzilopochtli. Montezuma was afraid. He had allowed Quetzalcoatl to return and didn't know what else to do. I was silent for a long time, not wanting to enrage Montezuma anymore. Finally he roused himself and to their great relief the messengers were released. "Maybe we can try one more thing. Call for more messengers and offer Cortez the god Quetzalcoatl gold to not come here. If he turns around now maybe the gods will not be offended and we can have peace." The envoys were sent straight away with the offer. I returned home to my house across the lake to await the results. I didn't bother to go back across the lake to wait for word. I knew that my runners, who I pay well to keep me informed, would bring me news. I was not to be disappointed. "The god known as Cortez received the envoys who offered him money to turn around. Cortez refused and told them that he looked forward to seeing Montezuma in Tenochtitlan and would leave then if asked." I immediately set out for the palace for I know that Montezuma would be calling for me to come. Montezuma wasted no time as I entered, "Stay here tonight and come with me tomorrow. I have sent Cacamatzin to the outskirts of the city to meet him and escort him to the city. From there I shall escort them to stay next to my palace. There we can keep an eye on them."

Outside Tenochtitlan
Esteban Speaks

We had slept well in a village outside the city called Ayotzinco and the morning of November 7 we were preparing to break camp when we heard the guard call out, "For the love of God. Look at that!" In the distance we could see brightly dressed men carrying a liter of gold and jewels. Cortez quickly ordered Malinche and Aguilar to the front of the army to serve as translators while he formed us in orderly lines to serve as both guard of honor and protection in case of a trap. The liter was carried into the midst of the army and I could see the look of lust on the soldier's faces as they stared at the gold liter. I'm sure the look of gold lust was on my face too. The liter was placed on the ground and a young man in a jeweled and decorated loin cloth and flowered cape stepped out, but not before the liter carriers had placed mats and flowers on the ground for him to step on. Cortez, sensing the importance of the occasion came forward and the man started the discourse that would be translated from Nahuatl to Mayan to Spanish. "I am Cacamatzin, nephew of the great Montezuma sent to escort you to greet him tomorrow as you enter the city. He is most sorry that he was not able to greet you here and hopes that my humble greetings will suffice."

We set out immediately. As we got closer we could see the beautiful city in the distance. Temple mounts could be seen through trees and the waters of the lake. We marched that day with Cacamatzin pointing out the different sights of the outskirts of the city. We were given a large lunch and proceeded on to pass the night in a huge and ornate compound with gardens, bathing areas and great rooms. This building in an area called Iztapalapan was nicer than anything I had seen in Cuba or Spain. Again Cortez set up guards for the night in case of subterfuge, but I slept well dreaming of gold and lands in the new world.

November 8, 1519 we awoke early to begin our march into Tenochtitlan. Cortez had arranged our parade to provide the most security and the biggest spectacle for the Mexicans. The horses came first to provide a sense of awe from the Mexicans who had never seen anything like them before. Next the soldiers marched in their best clothes and polished weapons. We crossed one bridge, which I suppose signified the entrance to the city when we saw another liter even grander than the one carrying Cacamatzin approach. This we knew had to be Montezuma and Cortez came forward to embrace him, but was stopped at the last minute. I assume this was because Montezuma could not be touched by a mere mortal. Montezuma looked at Cortez and through the usual translation ceremony he greeted Cortez with "How tired you must be to come to your land. It has been foretold that you should return and now here you are. Come. Rest and be happy." It sounded in the translation that Montezuma thought Cortez a god. I never could be sure what was being said by the time it has passed through to the third language. Cortez greeted him in the name of King Charles and then place a jeweled necklace over the head of Montezuma.

With the formal ceremonies over we marched the rest of the way through town and were placed in a beautiful palace adjacent to the palace of Montezuma. He had ordered supplies for us and women to cook our meals. The compound was large enough to house everyone. Us soldiers were housed in large rooms off a central courtyard. The natives had given us mats to sleep on and water jugs by the mats. The latrine was large pots in each room that were emptied almost immediately before there was a chance to smell. I went to sleep that night content, full, and happier than I had been since leaving Cuba.

The next morning I awoke and was so comfortable it took me a moment to realize where I was. I turned over and went back to sleep dreaming of gold. Suddenly I heard a sound from outside and jumped up, putting on my breeches as I ran to the door. Now fully dressed I stood on the street and saw a parade of naked men being led down the street toward the pyramid temple. It took me a moment to realize what was going on and then it hit me with dread. These men were being taken to the temple for sacrifice to their god. Just as I was wondering why they didn't try to escape one made a run for it. The man was dirty and muddy, but even with the mud he looked like he had a lighter complexion than the others. I realized with horror that he was a Spaniard! I started to shout for help and for the Mexica to stop when I realized the naked man being led to his death was Alejandro. The soldiers leading the parade easily threw ropes tied to stones and Alejandro was easily recaptured as the rope wrapped itself around his legs. My shouting had drawn the attention of the Mexica guards who surrounded me and clamped their hands over my mouth. Alejandro was then grabbed by two strong guards and they continued down the street. The men were pushed up the steep steps of the temple to stand in a group at the top. Alejandro was the first to go. He was thrown on top of a post the size of a dinner plate and held by four guards so that his legs and arms were held from below. The priest then held a dagger above his head and plunged it into his chest. The blood spurted as Alejandro cried out and the priest pulled the dagger out and with his other hand dove in to the chest to pull out the still beating heart. The priest held the heart up to the sun for a moment and threw it into a fire burning to one side. That part of the ritual over, the four men who were holding the now dead Alejandro, carried him by the arms and legs and threw the body down the steps of the pyramid. I felt sick to my stomach but couldn't keep my eyes off the spectacle. Men or priests at the bottom grabbed the body and chopped off the arms and legs and threw them into a pot of water and I realized they were going to eat the body. The skin was cut from Alejandro's body and placed like a cape around the body of a priest. All this was happening while at the top of the pyramid another man had met the same fate and his lifeless body was thrown down the steps. This continued on as twenty bodies were sacrificed and the heads placed on shelves at the bottom of the temple steps.

"It's terrible." I heard a voice say. I turned around and it was Martin. "I think it's worse than what we saw at the coast." He continued. "Why do they do that? Do they really think that gods need a human sacrifice?" Martin had been sleeping on the next mat and woke up at the same time. He came out just as Alejandro was captured after trying to escape. "Did you see how they caught him using the rope? I wonder why they don't try to escape?" I couldn't think of any reason, but said, "Maybe they really want to go. Maybe they give them something so they don't know what they're doing." Martin nodded his head. " Maybe they think that the next life will be better because they're getting killed." I agreed and we continued back to the compound.

We met Cortez at the door. He had heard the commotion and came outside to see what was going on. We quickly briefed him about what we had seen. He muttered an oath, "I suppose I should have expected that. What kind of people are these?" He resolved to talk to Montezuma about it when he met him again. We didn't have too long to wait. Montezuma came to visit Cortez in the morning bearing gifts of gold and jewels. He was accompanied by other men in liters dressed in extravagant loin cloths embroidered with jewels and golden threads. I saw the man, Cacamatzin, who had met us outside the city. I also saw another man who seemed important who was introduced as Montezuma's cousin Cuauhtémoc. The three way method of communication worked again, but I still wasn't sure I understood everything. Montezuma seemed to ask if Cortez was a god. I nearly laughed when I heard that, remembering the stories of Cortez leaping naked from a married woman's bedroom escaping a husband. As if reading my mind Cortez glared at me and replied, "I come from the great emperor Charles who desires to greet you as a brother." Montezuma said something that sounded like he wanted us to leave to which Cortez said "If you want us to leave after I have done my duty we shall, but my king will be upset that I have not made friends with you. I see that you sacrifice humans to your god. Why do you not sacrifice animals and birds?" When this was translated Montezuma said that animals were fine for some things such as the birds sacrificed to make sure that the sun came up every morning, but some things required human sacrifice. Cortez took this as an opportunity. "We come to tell you about the one God and his son Jesus Christ. Jesus was sacrificed once for our sins and he rose from the dead and calls all to become Christians. I desire that you become a Christian just like me. My king, the great Charles V, will send others to teach about Jesus. These others are much more knowledgeable than I." Montezuma paused and looked like he didn't want to talk about this. "Thank you for your many kind words. I hear that the women are preparing your lunch so I shall take my leave."

Tenochtitlan
Cuauhtémoc Speaks

The invader came with his army. I visited them this morning with Montezuma before lunch. They have a woman who speaks our language named Malinche. I don't think they know that her name means "Like a wild beast," and sure to cause problems. Let us hope that the problems

131

she causes are for them and not for us. She speaks our language and then tells a man what was said and he then tells the god Cortez. Cortez tried to tell us about his god who was sacrificed and that others would come to teach about this god. He then told the god king Montezuma that he wished Montezuma would become like him. This was an affront to Montezuma and Huitzilopochtli. The king was very patient in dealing with the invaders and left them to their meal. I look forward to the day when we shall see their bodies being thrown from the temple as a sacrifice to Huitzilopochtli.

Tencohtitlan

Esteban Speaks

We had been confined to the compound for several days. I didn't mind since my mind was still processing what I had seen at the temple. Martin and I spent time talking. He and Tomas, Diego and the other men that had specifically come and talked to me after I apologized were now pretty close. We had fought together through a couple battles and slogged through the freezing areas by the volcano. We had arranged our mats together in the large room of the compound. I don't know how the others felt, but I felt that they had forgiven me and we were now friends. I suppose fighting battles together does that. "Tomas, can I ask you something," I said. Then without waiting for a response I asked, "The day I asked everybody to forgive me you said that you had taken a belt to my ass because of anger. Were you more angry at me or our situation? I know you said it was because of the situation, but I want to know." He looked at me with a hard look and I thought I had overstepped what I thought was friendship. Then he softened, "At first, yes, I was angry with you. I've been at sea since I was 13. I've seen plenty of floggings for all kinds of reasons. A theft was pretty common to receive a flogging so I wasn't surprised. What did surprise me was that you were considered one of the elite." I started to argue, "No hear me out. You were an elite. You were a friend of Cortez and in charge of the money. If you were an officer you would have been second or third in command. I had never seen an officer accused of theft, much less be sentenced to flogging. When I saw that you had stolen from us I was angry at you, but also angry at the system. I knew that in all the years I had been at sea there couldn't have been every officer with clean hands. I knew that officers had gotten away with many things before with no consequences. When I saw you in the pillory I knew I had my chance to get back at every officer who had ever done anything wrong. Right or wrong I grabbed a belt and whipped your ass till it bled and I was satisfied." I looked at him in amazement. I suppose I had been an elite, but I never thought that he had taken his frustration of so many people out of me. I thanked him for being honest and tried to close with a joke, "I hope I never act like an officer to you agin." He smiled. "I think I probably need to ask your forgiveness. Yeah, you deserved a whipping, but I gave you more than you deserved." I thought through my past, "No. I think I probably deserved everything that was coming to me."

Several days later Cortez sent word to Montezuma that he would like to visit the city. I could see that Cortez was planning an eventual battle and so must know the city well. He asked to visit the tallest point around: a temple on the other side of the town. To my surprise Montezuma sent the man Cuauhtémoc to lead us. "My cousin has gone ahead to sacrifice so that the gods will not be unhappy to have you visit." My heart sank at the idea that somebody was being killed so that we could see the view. I prayed that the knowledge we learned could help to put an end to the killing. We walked across town carefully guarded by the native army, but not feeling threatened. Along the way Cuauhtémoc pointed out the sights of the city. I had noticed that the city did not have the smell of sewer like every city I have known. Human waste was not thrown in the streets to smell as it was at home in Spain or Cuba. Here the waste was collected and taken by canoe to the other side of the lake and dumped. The market here was larger than anything I had seen in Spain with so many things to purchase that I had never seen before. I was impressed and for the moment forgot about the sacrifices taking place so we could visit the temple.

It didn't take long to be brought back to memory. As we approached the temple we saw two bodies being thrown from the top of the temple. Montezuma stood at the top and called for us to come up. The steps up the pyramid were steep and several priests offered to help us up. I looked at the priest who was covered in dried blood from head to toe as well as the blood of the young man who lay dead at our feet and knew I could never let him touch me. We scrambled up the steps without the help of the priests and I tried to avoid the middle of the steps where most of the blood was. Montezuma greeted us warmly and showed us the view of the city from the top of the temple. "From here you can see the whole city. There is where you came in from outside the city. There is my palace and next to it is yours." He said with pride over the city Cortez spent some time looking at the city and I could tell he was thinking how he would do battle in the city.

Finally Cortez tore his eyes away from the view and asked of Montezuma if we could visit the rooms at the top of the temple. Montezuma talked briefly with the blood soaked priests and motioned for us to follow him. I was immediately sorry that I had been allowed to come. There were statues of gods that looked like snakes and blood everywhere. I could see human hearts on a shelf in front of one of the statues and I nearly retched. We didn't stay in the room long and I was glad to leave and wanted to head back to our temporary home. Cortez didn't leave so fast but casually asked "Why do you do this? You are a very brave and intelligent man. Do you not see that these gods are devils?" Montezuma looked angry but answered casually. "These are the gods and desire to be fed. If I had known that this is how you would act I wouldn't have invited you to the temple. I think it time that you go now. I must stay here to sacrifice more to appease the gods that you have insulted."

We made our way down the steps, but the priests had one more stop and showed us the room where the bodies were cut up and cooked. Again we saw more skulls arranged on shelves in front of us. I couldn't count the number of skulls and was glad to leave.

Tenochtitlan
Cuauhtémoc Speaks

The invaders show little respect for our religion or gods. Today the Cortez god asked to see the temple and we showed him the city and the temple. He was allowed to climb the sacred steps to the temple of Smoking Mirror and Hummingbird South. After he was allowed to see everything he had the audacity to tell Montezuma the god king that Smoking Mirror and Huitzilopochtli were devils and we should not sacrifice to them. Montezuma held his patience but was clearly angry. He suggested that Cortez return to the palace. Montezuma had to stay and sacrifice

more men to the two gods to mollify them for the behavior
of Cortez.

Tenochtitlan

Esteban Speaks

We arrived back "home," which was really another
palace down the street from Montezuma's palace. We had
been in the capital a week surrounded by a culture of
death. I was shaken and still retched at the memory of the
sight of the body being flung down the stairs of the temple.
I needed the comfort of something familiar and searched
for a church or chapel to pray. Of course that was not to be
found in this palace built around human sacrifice. I
mentioned this to several of the soldiers who had been on
the excursion to the temple, Diego and Gabriel. "Let's ask
the priest if we can set up a chapel and altar to Our Lady,"
suggested one soldier. We will look for an empty room
that will have space to worship. There were about five of
us who set out around the palace looking for a room where
we could set up an altar or a chapel with a picture of Our
Lady. The palace was huge with ample room for the
several hundred Spaniards who were now living there. We
toured corridors that connected to great rooms that joined
courtyards filled with trees and tropical birds. We went
down one corridor in the center of the palace complex and
one man said "Look how this hallway doesn't seem to

have any rooms off it." We searched the hallway and around the corner and found no doors to other rooms. It was at this point that one of the men said, "Look at this. It looks like fresh paint on the wall." Sure enough. The whole section of wall had fresh paint. Another looked at the floor and ceiling and said "Look here at the floor. Right there it looks like a door that has been walled up with fresh stucco and that's why the wall was repainted. There must be a room behind this wall." We took it open ourselves to pry apart the area that looked like a joint and discovered the stucco easily falling apart to reveal a large room off the hall. Someone brought a candle and my heart leapt at the sight of gold.

"We must get Cortez," I said. "We dare not go in there or touch anything without him going in first. I don't want to repeat my time in the pillory." Leaving the others to guard the opening I ran to find Cortez and quickly told him what we had found. He arrived at the opening and went in first. We followed with torches and I was dazzled at the amount of gold and jewels in this room. It was more than could be imagined and more than any of us had ever seen in our lives. Cortez looked through the whole room and I wondered if he was thinking about the second set of books I had started and if he could keep news of this from the king. "I must have this treasure." He announced. "It must belong to the King. And us."

From there he commenced to plan on how to take over and control the city and by default all the tribes under control of Montezuma. Then came bad news from Vera Cruz. One of the Mexican mayors had gone to our first allies the Totonacs and demanded taxes. The chief of the Totonacs had then gone to Vera Cruz seeking our help since Cortez had promised help if they allied with us. The soldiers remaining in Vera Cruz had provided help, but they had only been the older soldiers left to defend the city and several were killed. "This will help us," declared Cortez, when he heard the news and requested to meet with Montezuma.

"You have betrayed our friendship." Cortez bluntly told Montezuma. "You have gone to war and allowed my friends to be killed with the Totonacs." Montezuma quickly denied everything but sent out runners to bring the mayor from the coast to Tenochtitlan. "He shall be judged and punished," assured Montezuma. "We are still friends." Cortez continued with his plan. "Oh your Majesty. The way you can assure our friendship is to leave this palace and come next door to my palace and stay with me." Montezuma looked shocked. "I could never do that. My people would demand that I stay in my palace." Cortez had an answer for that. "No Your Majesty. It would be exactly as if you were here. Your people could continue to come and visit you and you could do all your work. It would just be doing it in another location." Montezuma tried several times to get out of it, but finally he agreed to move over to our palace.

Tenochtitlan
Cuauhtémoc Speaks

The Cortez god has asked my cousin to move to his palace. My cousin doesn't want to, but the Cortez god insisted. He really had no choice when a god requests something. He has been allowed movement in and out of the palace and I and the others have been allowed to visit. Montezuma declared that he was happy to spend some time with Cortez and we should not worry. I see the end in this. Cortez god has taken control of my cousin and soon he will control the city and land.

Tenochtitlan
Esteban Speaks

Montezuma has moved to our palace. We have been given instructions that we are to treat him with great respect and he is to continue his life as he normally would. There are guards around him all the time. We are not to limit his access to anything, or even his ability to leave. We are just to guard him or the doors to his section of the compound. I try to get on guard duty with with Diego, Tomas or Martin. They are the closest I have to friends right now. Some of the men ignore me while others talk briefly and go on. Martin and I were standing guard outside the door and I decided to ask Martin why he was willing to forgive me too. "I've heard what Diego told you, that he was flogged for stealing too. Tomas told me that he was getting back at every officer who had wronged him. I guess I don't have that good a reason. I just figured it was the right thing to do. The priest tells us to forgive so I guess I have to forgive. Maybe the hardest person to get forgiveness from is yourself." That stopped me in my tracks. Had I forgiven myself? Did I still even think that I had done something wrong? Sure I had the scars on my back and ass to remind me that I had done something wrong, but did I really feel it? After all I had convinced myself it was ok to steal from the church by saying that we needed it. I had also convinced myself that the two sets of books were necessary to raise money to go on the expedition. I also told myself that two books were a common thing in accounting. Maybe I hadn't even admitted to myself that I had done something wrong.

A move in the hall brought me back to the present. Somebody was here to see Montezuma. We were not allowed to interfere in any way. In this case it was that Cuauhtémoc who is related somehow. He comes in barefoot and does not look Montezuma in the eyes. They must think that Montezuma is a god. Everything here looks so strange. I suppose if we brought Montezuma to Spain everything would look strange to him too. I know when my father goes before the king he makes sure to not turn his back on him and always bows. Maybe things aren't so different after all.

All his people come and go as normal and he eats his meals as normal. Anybody visiting him comes before him without sandals and does not look him in the eye. He eats apart from anyone else behind a screen and only eats what his women prepare. After being out to the temple I knew that the priests ate human flesh. I don't know if Montezuma is required to do the same. I do not know if he eats men who have been sacrificed to their god, but I do not want to see what the women are cooking. I purposefully avoid the area where the women do the cooking.

Montezuma had only been with us about a week when the mayor of the city that attacked Vera Cruz was brought before Montezuma. He didn't spend too much time with Montezuma before he was brought over to Cortez and sentenced to death. Cortez ordered a fire built in the courtyard and Montezuma chained. The Mayor was brought out in chains and thrown into the fire. Montezuma was forced to watch and did nothing. I realized then that Cortez had effectively gained control of the city and Montezuma was forced to be a puppet ruler.

Now that Montezuma lived with us Cortez and he had plenty of time to talk and work together. They played games and talked about religion. Everybody from Cortez to all the soldiers seemed to like Montezuma.

Malinche and Aguilar are always included in these conversations until Aguilar learns the language of the Mexica or Montezuma learns Spanish. One day they hung around the door after Cortez had left and I took a moment to ask Malinche about her life. "I know you have lived at the beach. Where did you learn the language?" If she was surprised that a man would ask her a question she didn't show it. "I was born at the sea and given away by my mother to another tribe. That is where I learned the language." I was astounded that a mother would give away her daughter and asked "Why were you given away?" "Why? Why does the sun rise? Why do flowers grow? That is the way of life. Men go to war and women get pulled away from family and sold as slave or given for sex. Women must accept what is placed before them. Sometimes women find a way above where they are placed." I thought about the woman who was given to me by Cortez. I didn't know her name when I took her into the brush within 5 minutes after she was given to Cortez. One moment she was at the side of her mother and a few minutes later I was fucking her on the sand. I wondered if that woman would find anything better in life. I had deflowered her and she had been passed around since then between Santiago and Mateo and now who knows how many other men. Malinche had made the best of her situation. She had been given to Cortez as a concubine, but when she saw her chance to improve her lot by translating she had grabbed it. She might always be a concubine, but for now she had some power as no man would dare take Cortez' concubine. I wondered how much longer before she would be pregnant with Cortez' child or the child of whoever he decided to give her to. I thought briefly about how I treated women. Certainly I treated my mother with respect. I treated Maria, the wife of the mayor, with respect but I wanted sex. The other women around had been sex objects that I gained by throwing some coins on the bed, or in the case of the woman I just took. In fact, the last woman I had taken was a few days previous in an empty room of the compound. She was in the center courtyard when I was outside. She had looked at me and I decided that I wanted her. I don't know if she agreed, she just accepted what was happening to her. I wondered how many of the women I had taken had borne children.

Soon after that we heard a rumor that involved Cacamatzin, the man who had originally escorted us from outside the city to meet Montezuma. He was of another tribe and Cortez believed the rumors that he was planning on using the uncertainty surrounding Montezuma to try and take over the city and the Mexican valley. We set up a plan that made it seem to Cacamatzin that he had support from some of the locals. He was encouraged to come to a meeting in a building by the lake with these "supporters." Diego, Martin, Tomas and I were part of the group that was sent to the building by the lake. There were about 15 or 20 natives in the large room who had all sworn allegiance to Montezuma, and by extension, Cortez.

Cacamatzin had been informed that several local notables wanted to meet him, but they couldn't meet him near the palace for obvious reasons. The lake house was chosen because it was away from the city by the mainland only accessible by canoe. Malineche and Aguilar stayed away and so us four Spaniards were only able to communicate by sign language or our limited Nuhuatl. We had all been briefed with what to do. The Spaniards were there only to arrest Cacamatzin in the name of Cortez. The natives met us at our compound in canoes and Diego and I started enter with chains to bind Cacamatzin once he was captured. One of the natives looked at us and shook his head. I couldn't understand till finally Malinche and Aguilar were brought out. "He says that you shouldn't wear those clothes. You will be seen too easily and there is no place to hide you at the lake house." Our clothes were quickly shed and replaced with loincloths and dirt rubbed on our faces and chests to make us appear darker. We entered the canoes one more time with the native rowers and chains. Once we got to the lake house I understood why we weren't allowed to wear our normal clothes. The room was large, but we would have stood out in our clothes. The room was accessed by a ladder from the lake to a hole in the floor of the house. It was the only entrance to the house so it was a perfect ambush. A couple peep holes were quickly made in the walls to see when Cacamatizin would come. Our canoes were left under the lake house to show that we were here. In the moonlight we could soon see two incoming canoes. Cacamatzin was coming, but with only two canoes we had him outnumbered. The Spaniards were sent to the back of the room so that we would blend in with all the others. Martin and I had carried the chains up through the hole earlier and they now lay on the floor behind us ready to chain Cacamatzin. Tomas looked out through one of the peepholes and announced "Makuili tlakatl" very proud of his ability to say 'five men' in Nuhautl. The other men chuckled at his attempt to speak Nuhuatl. Soon we heard the sound of the two canoes scraping the ground under the house and and the crunch of pebbles as the five men exited the canoes. One of the locals stuck his head out of the hole and shouted something that we assumed meant "Come on up." We were at the rear of the room and so couldn't see who came up first, but the natives had it all arranged. As each man came up the hole he was surround by two or three natives who waited till Cacamatzin came up last before attacking. The natives pulled small knives out of the back of their loincloths and each man was quickly subdued. Cacamatzin's four helpers didn't put up too much of a fight as they were easily outnumbered. Cacamatzin was grabbed as his head and arms appeared through the hole. Two men grabbed his arms and pulled him the rest of the way through the hole while another two men grabbed his legs with a scream. Cacamatzin struggled and shouted something. The natives just laughed at whatever he had said and Cacamatzin struggled all the more trying to release himself from the four men. Finally he was subdued, but in the process his loincloth had torn off and he was carried naked toward us at the back of the room. I had the brief thought that he looked like one of the men being carried to the sacrificial stone, except he was being sacrificed to Cortez, King Charles and the conquest. When he saw us and realized we were Spaniards in loincloths he shouted and struggled again to no avail. It was all over in a moment. Diego and I helped hold down Cacamatzin, while Tomas and Martin chained him. The four other men were threatened with knives and their hands tied behind their backs with their own loincloths. The five men were dragged to the hole and roughly shoved and dropped to the ground below to the waiting arms of the men who had exited first. We threw the men in to the canoes and set off across the lake to our compound which now served as the palace of Cortez, the ruler of Mexico. Cortez, Aguilar and Malinche were waiting in his "throne" room as we brought the struggling five men before him. He dealt with the four aides first. "You shall be released to the locals to be dealt with for your insurrection against Montezuma." When the men heard that they moaned for Montezuma was popular still with the people even though he was imprisoned in Cortez' compound. "We shall be killed," one moaned. Cortez said nothing and they were led away to what I assumed was the local version of police. I was certain their heads would be on a shelf in the temple before morning. Cortez then turned his attention to Cacamatzin. "You have risen against your rightful leader Montezuma. You should be put to death, but in light of your royal heritage I sentence you to be chained in the compound here for life." Cacamatzin struggled against his chains, but he too was pulled from the room. Cortez looked at us and said "Thank you for your work tonight." I realized we were still in our loincloths when he continued, "Are you trying to turn native?"

It seemed that Cortez was in charge. Montezuma and he seemed to be very friendly, but the shift of power was evident. The next plan was to work on having Montezuma swear allegiance to Charles. With Cacamatzin out of the way and always the chance that another could take his place Cortez started pressuring Montezuma to swear allegiance to Charles. Once while Tomas and I were stationed inside the door as we usually did when Cortez and Montezuma were in conference we heard part of the exchange, "Sire in order for us to be closer as brothers and friends you need to swear allegiance to my king Charles." Montezuma made some kind of comment how he and Cortez were already close and he didn't need to swear allegiance to another king. The gods would not allow it. Cortez replied that the Lord Jesus Christ required it, but that made no difference to Montezuma. This went on for some days till finally Montezuma said, "Enough Cortez god. I will do what you want." Cortez was happy and sent me to get a priest and one of the ship officers. The ceremony was the next day where in front of a priest to perform a mass and the ship's officer who served as a notary Montezuma swore allegiance to Charles. I remembered that the notary was the same who witnessed the making of Vera Cruz as a city. With incense and chants the paperwork was made official and Mexico was a vassal state of Spain.

He assumed that by this time Charles had received the documents making Vera Cruz a city under Charles. If Cortez could have Montezuma swear allegiance to Charles then Charles would have a whole new nation and Cortez hoped that he would be made governor.

Tenochtitlan
Cuauhtémoc Speaks

The Cortez god has pushed and pushed my cousin ever since Cacamatzin was captured to swear allegiance to this other king across the seas. I don't know if any of us understand who this king is. Montezuma called the senior leaders and family to tell us he had decided to accept the terms of allegiance. We agreed that he could do whatever he wanted since Quetzalcoatl did work with other gods and if Cortez was a god it must be Quetzalcoatl returned. I agreed with the others and with Montezuma, but in the back of my mind I agreed with the understanding that we had plenty of soldiers to take out the Cortez god if need be.

The next day Montezuma signed the document in their strange writing that doesn't use pictures as our writing does. The Cortez god had his priests chanting things about a woman "mother of god" and her son. It all sounded so strange to me. They used their priests, but Montezuma was not allowed to have his own priests make sacrifice to ease the god's anger.

Although the people had not been told what was going on it seemed that everyone know. Mexicans across the city were upset, not knowing what the future held. There was a continuous parade of people leaving the city to join family in the country.

Some time after that Montezuma asked permission to mount the temple to tell the people that he still worshipped the gods and they should not worry. Cortez agreed as long as no one was sacrificed. Montezuma left the palace of Cortez in his liter wearing his finest clothes and arrived at the temple. Montezuma did not sacrifice anyone, but the priests did to make sure that the gods were happy. The white men have not climbed the temple ever since that first week when they did and Montezuma and the gods were offended.

Tenochtitlan
Esteban Speaks

Things had settled down after Montezuma swore allegiance to Charles. The soldiers and Cortez enjoyed his company. Sometimes they took excursions around the city or lake. I don't know if Montezuma ever figured out that the excursions were really so that Cortez could understand the city and plan for a fight if he needed to leave or put up a battle to defend the new colony of Spain.

Montezuma seemed to like Cortez and us soldiers. He often roamed the compound using his simple Spanish words while we tried the few Nuhuatl words we had learned. When he was with us he was a normal man and , although we treated him with great respect due a king, he treated us almost as friends. Once on his walk through the compound he saw me in the courtyard working with my shirt off. He looked at the scars on my back and commented, "You bad?" I smiled at his words while Tomas and Diego howled with laughter. "Notoka Amokuali Iyouilia," and it was Montezuma's turn to laugh. In my simple Nahuatl I had said "My name is bad person. I punished without pity." I suppose that was the truth. One day he came to where we were working and he called me by his new name for me "Amokuali, you get Cortez god." I understood that he wanted to speak to Cortez so I ran off in search of him. "Sir. His Majesty Montezuma wishes to speak to you. He sent me here from the courtyard," Cortez looked up from the papers on his desk. "So I understand he has an appropriate name for you?" I blushed at the reminder of my flogging and time in the pillory. Although Cortez was magnanimous after he freed me from the pillory he hadn't let me forget that I once had been a trusted aide and had brought my new low status on through my own fault. "Yes sir. I told him that I was punished." I added, without need, "it was my own fault." Cortez grunted and said, "Ok. Take me to Montezuma. Let's see what he wants."

I brought Cortez to Montezuma and watched as Montezuma led Cortez through the courtyard. He looked at us men and said, "You boys come." Finally we were brought to the wall where we had discovered the gold. "I am giving all of this to you." He said. We were shocked by his generosity. I wondered if he knew that Cortez was planning on taking it anyway. "We give you thanks," said Cortez, trying to avoid looking shocked. I just stood there thinking about my two books that lay on a beach in Vera Cruz. I thought back to when one of the envoys asked Cortez if he would take gold in exchange for leaving and wondered if this was why Montezuma was giving us gold.

Of course Cortez had made no attempt to hide his hatred of human sacrifice and the Mexican religion. He had spent much time talking with Montezuma about Our Lady and finally came to a decision that she must have a place in the city. This time Diego and I were standing guard inside the door "I want to place a cross and a picture of Our Lady in the temple. Our Lady must be the Queen of Mexico," came the request. Montezuma might have sworn allegiance to Charles, but he wasn't going to give up his entire culture easily."I can't allow you to do that. The gods will be unhappy and the people will suffer," was the response. "Then we might have to do it ourselves and throw down some gods," Cortez threatened. This went on for several days and finally Montezuma said that the priests had given permission for a chapel to be built. I was given the job to lead the group to the temple and prepare it for consecration as a chapel to Our Lady with the words from Cortez, "Do it quickly so we can celebrate mass there tomorrow." I wondered if I was being given this job because Cortez now trusted me or because if the priests rebelled my death would be little mourned among the Spaniards. I finally decided it was the latter. We arrived at the temple and started to climb the steep steps. I warned the men what we would see at the top since I was the only one who had been there before. "It is pure evil up there. It is covered with blood of those sacrificed to a pagan god. We must prepare it for use to our Lord and Savior Jesus Christ." I concluded that we needed to pray before we climbed any further. If the men thought it strange that I required them to pray before ascending they didn't argue and we paused for a moment in prayer. When we arrived at the top after walking through the last steps that were coated with the blood of victims I heard some men retching. We tore down the few statues that we could move easily and threw them down the steps. When everything was removed that we could easily move we made a chain gang of men hauling soap and water up the steps so we could clean everywhere on the top and then worked at cleaning blood from the steps all the way down. Once finished we cleaned out the area beneath where the skulls were stored. Again as we cleared the area I heard retching from the men that didn't stop until we had cleared out enough skulls that the breeze was able to clear the air of death. I sent the skulls to a grassy area nearby where I had the men dig a hole deep enough for all the skulls. We worked all day and into the night by torch light before we realized we had to go home and let the temple air out. "I'm dead." I announced as we got back to the compound. "I want to soak this smell of death off me." The four of us found one of the ponds in the compound, throwing our clothes to one side jumped in to soak away the smell and memory of what we had done today. "Do you think it will be clean enough for the priest tomorrow? Asked Tomas. "I hope so. We couldn't work anymore. We'll let the night air blow through. Maybe it will be better in the morning. I don't relish the idea of getting back in those clothes tomorrow. I think they should be burned too!"

The next morning we were up early and walked the short distance to the temple. We were pleased with our work from the previous day. The soap and water we had used cleaned off the blood except for that that had just permeated the stone and it looked just like dark stone. The room at the top had been cleaned out and an altar had been placed ready for the Eucharist. The room at the bottom of the temple where the skulls had been placed on shelves smelled clean and looked like it could be ready as a chapel. As a group we walked back to the compound and told Cortez and the waiting priests that the new chapel was ready for consecration. We soldiers were given the honor of carrying the cross and a picture of the Blessed Virgin up the street in the procession. As the priest chanted "Lord Have Mercy" I reflected on how far I had come.

Tenochtitlan
Cuauhtémoc Speaks

They have desecrated the temple by knocking down one of the gods and placing a picture of their woman god in its place. This cannot continue. Smoking Mirror god will be upset. I have sent my runners across the lake to talk to the priests and made arrangements for them to bring back some of the priests to my lakeside house. I think I will have the runners make sure they are cleaned of blood before they come.

"Oh great priest of the eternal Smoking Mirror. What does Smoking Mirror tell you?" I had had the runners bring two of the priests back across the lake and had attendants help them bathe and provided them with new clothing and a generous contribution in the hopes that I could bend them to my will. In the end I needn't have bothered. Smoking Mirror was angry at Cortez and the white men. "Smoking Mirror says that the white men have angered him and he will not be happy until the white men are dead. We are going to tell Montezuma that he must go to war against the white men and drive them from our country." I smiled to myself. This is turning out easy. If the priests tell Montezuma that Smoking Mirror has declared that the white men must go then he would be forced to take action. I must go across the lake so that I happen to be there when they make their presentation.

Tenochtitlan
Esteban Speaks

"Now that the Virgin is installed in the temple things will settle down." I said to no one in particular. "No. We are at the mercy of Montezuma," came the response from Cortez. I didn't even know he was in the room. "If something happens to him we have no protection. We must be prepared for anything."

At that point an aide came to Cortez and said "His Majesty Montezuma wishes to talk with you." I was on guard duty with Martin at the time and so we went on to Montezuma while Tomas went in search of Malinche and Aguilar. We arrived to find Montezuma looking somewhat perturbed. Cortez invited me to go with him while he met with Montezuma. "The Lord Smoking Mirror has determined that you must leave the city. You have desecrated the temple and must leave." I understood Smoking Mirror to be another god, but I never did understand which god was which in the whole Mexica pantheon. Cortez was taken aback at the suddenness of the statement. "Well, Your Majesty. We can certainly leave, but we have no means to go. I must send some of my men to the woods to cut trees to make ships to leave." I thought he was bargaining for extra time, but Montezuma was ready. "I will send men to help you so you can leave soon."

Things went from bad to worse as news came that my Uncle had sent ships to search for and arrest Cortez. Somehow he had heard that we had declared the city of Vera Cruz and pushed him out of taking money from the expedition. I now had to face a problem. Do I cast my lot in with Cortez or take off with my uncle's crew and hope that Cortez is arrested and I get both my share of the gold and a share from my uncle. Cortez did not help me in my deliberations. I think he secretly enjoyed watching my torment. Word came from Vera Cruz that soldiers had arrived and set off to see Cortez. Several men were sent from the shore to demand that Cortez surrender. They certainly had it easier than when we came. Guides carried them non stop from the sea in liters and Cortez met them outside the city. They were given the best rooms in our palace and shown around the city. Cortez let them see the gold that had been given us and gave each of them some gold. They were sent back to the sea to tell the ship captains how rich they all were and how there was really no point in trying to arrest Cortez.

Montezuma's runners, having been bribed to report everything to Cortez first, came to say that the captains had ordered the soldiers to come to the city and capture Cortez. We were ordered out of the city with enough left to guard Montezuma. We headed for the city of Cempoalan where the army had taken control. Cortez ordered cannon fired at the temple where the soldiers had taken refuge and we surrounded the city and temple. Here he took a gamble that the soldiers knew nothing that Cortez had asked the King to declare him governor of the city. He loudly announced that any soldier who did not surrender did so on the threat of death for violating the trust that King Charles had placed in Cortez as governor of Mexico. In the end it was over before it really started. The soldiers began surrendering to Cortez and pledging allegiance to Cortez as governor. Cortez never left the highlands, but sent soldiers to take the ships with orders that they not return to Cuba. Our army was now larger than ever and my decision had been made for me. I was now 100% on the side of Cortez.

On the way back to the city we received news that there had been a scuffle during one of the many religious ceremonies that the Mexica have and several people were killed. Mexica soldiers surrounded the palace and refused to let the Spanish soldiers leave. Montezuma sent word that he had tried to pacify the people, but they were upset. Cortez wasted no time and returned to the city by way of one of the many bridges that allowed access to the city.

Tenochtitlan
Cuauhtémoc Speaks

My cousin has lost status and face among the people. Cortez returned to the city after fighting the bandits from the east who came to arrest him. That was his mistake. The people no longer care to provide meals or supplies to the invader. Montezuma is alone in the palace while others prepare for a battle against the invader. I am not taking up arms against my cousin, but I have ordered that the bridges connecting the city to the lake shore be raised and canoes be ready with soldiers so that the invader cannot escape without casualties. We must capture all the invaders so they can make the journey to top of the temple and the sacrificial stone and dagger. Smoking Mirror and Huitzilopochtli must be made happy. Cortez tried to leave several times with his army or part of his army. Each time his soldiers were turned back and some killed. I have moved myself closer to town to direct the soldiers under my command. I have ordered them to not fight my cousin, but only the invader. Today I watched as Mexica soldiers surrounded the palace that Cortez has been using and where he has Montezuma imprisoned. The soldiers began throwing rock and spears at □ □the palace knowing well that they couldn't take the palace. Unfortunately Montezuma chose this time to come out from the palace and stand on the wall to try and talk to the Mexica. He came out dressed in his ceremonial loincloth and feathered cape and tried to tell everyone to leave. Some soldiers had the nerve to shout at the man who they wouldn't have dared look at a few weeks ago, "We have elected a new leader. You no longer speak for us." More stones were thrown and one hit Montezuma and he fell behind the wall."

Escape

The Palace
Esteban Speaks

I am afraid for my life. Cortez has sent out various groups to find a way out of the city and each time they have returned with fewer men. Montezuma seemingly gave up hope working with Cortez who treated him poorly when he came back to the city. After we got back to the compound I heard Cortez berating Montezuma for the poor treatment we now received. Among Spaniards he called Montezuma a "dog" who didn't hunt. Montezuma tried to diffuse the situation by going out on the wall and calling to his people. What they answered I didn't know because Malinche was not there to translate. I did hear that the soldiers outside replied something and soon more stones were thrown. A stone hit Montezuma square in the head and he fell from the wall. Tomas and Diego were the closest to where he fell and came immediately to his side. They stayed by his side with tears in their eyes while he was carried back to his quarters. He lasted long enough for Cortez to visit and died. I felt as if my own father had died. I felt surrounded with no chance of escape from the city. In the sunset I could see the pyramid across the city. In the fading sunlight I saw the sacrificial stone shining with reflected sun. I felt my stomach drop as I imagined myself being stretched naked across the stone with a dagger held by a bloody priest above my chest.

On June 30 we made our attempt to flee. The gold had been separated with the King's fifth held out. The rest was given to us with what we could carry. I chose to carry very little, valuing my life more than gold. We tried to escape with soldiers, hostages and the women who had been given to us. I was in the front of the parade that tried to leave the city. We fought our way across several of the bridges and we were separated from the others. Behind us about half of the army was stuck behind a broken bridge. We fought our way forward across the rest of the bridges. Behind us I heard cries of my fellow soldiers as they were captured and dragged away. In my limited Nuhautl I heard the Mexicans shout about taking them to be sacrificed and drinking their blood. My heart sank as I thought about what they faced

We fought our way off the bridges till we made it to land. From there we were stuck. Behind us was the city of Tenochtitlan and the gold we had left behind. Ahead of us and what had taken weeks of travel was Vera Cruz and the ships waiting for us. The Mexica army could pick us off as easily as they wanted.

"Can we make it to Tlaxcala?" I asked Cortez. Tlaxcala had helped us but they were a week away at least. "Possibly," replied Cortez, "We don't have much of a choice. If they will help us we might be able to get to Vera

Cruz. If not we fight behind us and ahead of us." I knew what the lay ahead for us if captured.

Tenochtitlan
Cuauhtémoc Speaks

Montezuma is dead and we had a new elected leader who had been elected while Montezuma was held hostage. Cuitlahuac ordered the battle against Cortez. We fought the invader out of the city and on to the bridges to the mainland. Smoking Mirror was with us as we took down a bridge and divided Cortez from his army. Our soldiers were able to capture nearly half of his army while he fled with the other half. Our soldiers took the 800 men back to the temple so they could be sacrificed to Smoking Mirror and Huitzilopochtli. It took time that could have been used to finish off the army, but it was important to make the gods happy. The skulls were placed in boxes on the route to the city as a warning. The skin was flayed from the bodies so the priest could wear it till it fell apart.

The Escape Route
Esteban Speaks

We worked our way forward toward Tlaxcala ever waiting to hear the sound of approaching soldiers from Tenochtitlan. They never came and I don't know why. It would have been easy for them to repair the bridge they had destroyed to block our way and then follow us to land and capture us at will. I worked my way around the army to see if I could find Martin, Diego, Tomas and Gabriel. I found them and heaved a sigh of relief. In the distance I saw Mateo and was glad that he had made it.. Not seeing Santiago I asked somebody if they knew. "Yes. He was leading a group in the last part of the army. He was captured just as he was going to escape across the bridge. I saw them carry him above their heads as they headed back to town and the temple. It was terrible.I saw him and he looked brave. I don't think I would be brave."

We had escaped the city but Tlaxcala was a long way away.

I began to think that we could make it to Tlaxcala where, hopefully, they still wished to ally themselves with us. My hopes were dashed as we came over a hill and before us near the village of Otumba stood the armies of Mexica dressed in their finest war clothes. They had left Tenochtitlan by another route and stood before us ready to do battle. Again I had visions of the sacrificial stone. Cortez ordered an attack by the horsemen with a quick retreat so the soldiers could come in while the Mexica were reorganizing after the attack. This went on all day. I was an infantry soldier so I and others followed close to a group of five horsemen who attacked. Although the horses were no longer an oddity in Mexico the Mexica soldiers still ran and tried to avoid the flailing hooves and riders' swords. While the Mexica tried to regroup after the initial attack we foot soldiers attacked with sword to make a double attack. This went on all day with our fear of the sacrificial stone and dagger bringing us to new heights of courage. Finally in the later afternoon Cortez had ordered a special effort to attack anyone wearing brightly colored clothing assuming that they would be leaders. From somewhere while Cortez was attacking a spear came from the crowd of Spaniards and a soldier wearing brightly colored clothing fell dead. It was almost immediately that the whole battle changed. Some Mexica soldiers ran, while the leaders seemed to pull back from the battle and bring their soldiers with them. We were finally left alone on the battlefield with nothing separating us from Tlaxcala except mountains. I hoped that Tlaxcala still supported us. Otherwise a grim future awaited.

Otumba
Cuauhtémoc Speaks

We have failed. We had taken all the captured soldiers to be sacrificed to Huitzilopochtli and Smoking Mirror. From there we marched to Otumba to attack again and finish off the invader. It was a long day as they attacked with horses and swords. They targeted the leaders and, although I was able to kill some of the invader I was unable to kill Cortez. In the afternoon while I was fighting alongside Serpent Woman, the commander of the forces, a spear came from the invaders and impaled itself in the chest of Serpent Woman. I knew then the battle was over. Obviously we had done something wrong so that Smoking Mirror had abandoned us. Maybe we hadn't sacrificed enough of their soldiers, although nearly 800 had met the sacred stone. Maybe Smoking Mirror left us when we elected a new leader before Montezuma died while he was still a hostage of the invaders. Maybe Smoking Mirror left us when he first appeared as an old man when the invader was still marching on the city. Now it didn't matter. Serpent Woman was dead and the soldiers had seen him fall before their eyes. There would be no more stomach for war and they would flee. I reluctantly ordered my soldiers to retreat and go to their homes. I myself set back for my lakeside home to ponder what had happened to my country.

Tlaxcala
Esteban Speaks

We arrived in Tlaxcala July 12, 1520 to the sound of cheers. The Tlaxcalans brought us food and cared for our wounded. If I had doubted the generosity of the Tlaxcalans it was completely removed. For the first time in months I felt totally at peace and safe.

We settled in to relax and heal while Cortez planned. There was no option for retreat to Cuba or Spain for him.

He really had no choice. Although he had pretty much beat my uncle by appealing to the King and taking my uncle's ships and crew he had nothing to show for it. If he retreated to Cuba my uncle would throw him in jail and confiscate what little gold was left. If Cortez skipped Cuba and sailed directly to Spain the King would ask where the promised gold and colony was. If Cortez was unable to turn over gold and territory he might not be jailed, but would lose all access to the crown and influence at court. Cortez planned his final invasion of Mexico with care.

If we were to invade Tenochtitlan again we would need more supplies. Cortez brought me before him, "Esteban, you have become a trusted soldier. I thought that I might have to order your execution as a warning to others after I discovered your two accounting books." I blushed at the memory and also in thanks for the rare praise. "Thank you sir for giving me the chance. I knew after the pillory that my options were with you or the noose. Then when we got to Tenochtitlan I discovered my options were you or the stone." Cortez chuckled at the comparison. "We all fought with fear of what could happen on top of the pyramid. I pray for the souls daily of those captured and killed. We shall return to Mexico and this time we will conquer. For that we need supplies." I replied, "Yes sir. The Tlaxcalans have offered us help." "True," came the reply, "but we need supplies from Vera Cruz and more soldiers to return and fight. We have only just over 400 men and no gunpowder. I am sending you back to Vera Cruz with soldiers to bring back what men can be spared from there as well as all the supplies you can bring. I will send a list of what we need as well as letters that will eventually get to the king. I will also send what gold we were able to save from the treasure room. This must go to the king." He left unsaid what would happen to me if the gold or I were to disappear. I had seen the pillory and the stone.

I was placed in charge of the group going to the coast. Cortez leading a Tlaxcalan army went halfway with us to set up a new safe town so we and others could have an easy return to Tlaxcala. "We must have easy access to Vera Cruz and the sea if we expect to win. Vera Cruz will be the point of entry to New Spain, but Mexico will be the capital. When we take Tenochtitlan and the valley of the Mexica we take everything." He told us as we left.

I left with 50 soldiers to fight if needed, but mainly to put up a good show for all the villages between here and the sea. It took us nearly a week to make it to Vera Cruz. I had forgotten the heat and humidity of the sea and I perspired as we worked our way closer to sea level. We arrived to surprise from the older soldiers who had been left to keep Vera Cruz as a city for the king.

Over dinner that evening I regaled them with stories of what we had gone through. No matter that we had all seen a sacrifice so long ago with the Totanacs, every time I retell the story of the sacrifices we witnessed in Tenochtitlan I feel sick with grief. The mood was somber after dinner as the leader of the local guards said "We will find what supplies we can. The ships that Velazquez sent searching for Cortez are still here. We will empty the ships of anything we can use to take the country."

The next morning one of the guards reported seeing a ship on the horizon. We immediately prepared arms in case we had to fight again. My uncle, having sent two ships for Cortez without hearing from them, might have sent another ship. We were in luck. It was another ship from my uncle. As the crew came ashore they were greeted with muskets and threats of death. "What is the meaning of this?" asked the captain. "We come to take Cortez and see what has happened to the other ships." The "mayor" of Vera Cruz replied. "This is now the free city of Vera Cruz under grant from the crown. We need supplies and men." The ship was searched and anything that could be useful in the taking of Mexico was removed. The ship was sent on its way under the belief that king Charles had granted the rights of the city to Cortez.

We were preparing to return to Tlaxcala with more men and supplies when the guard came again,"There's a ship on the horizon." We watched as it came closer to shore. "It looks like a trade ship, not a war ship." Said the mayor. "I wonder who it is?" He was right. It was a trade ship from Spain that had been on its way to Cuba but blown off course. "We thought we were on course for Cuba but saw the shore and thought to investigate." The captain told us. "What do you carry?" I asked, hoping it would be of use. "We carry gunpowder, muskets and crossbows. Enough to start a revolution." I smiled. "Captain. We are going to be doing good business."

In the end it was good negotiating that helped us. I looked at the pillory standing before me and the king's fifth safely hidden in the storage room behind me and made a decision . We purchased everything on the ship using some gold from the king's fifth and gold that I was able to browbeat from the soldiers. I turned over the little amount of gold that I had been carrying in a bag around my neck and told the others. "We are doing this for the King." I sent the ship back to Spain with instructions to not stop in Cuba, but to go directly to Spain and deliver the letters that Cortez had written directly to the king. The captain promised and we continued to prepare for our march back to Tlaxcala. I hoped that Cortez would not place me in stocks again for using some of the king's gold to purchase firearms and gunpowder.

Happy with our purchases we left Vera Cruz with more supplies than Cortez could have dreamed of and about 100 extra soldiers. Cortez was going to have to try and take a nation with 500 men. As we got closer to Tlaxcala I began to worry about what I had done. Taking from the King's fifth was punishable by a brutal flogging, but I was pretty certain we needed the supplies, and I had taken from the soldiers too. I decided to tell Cortez the whole truth and hope that I could avoid death and maybe only serve time in the pillory again. "And so sir, I convinced the men to give me all the gold they had carried out of the treasure room and it still wasn't enough to buy all the supplies on the ship. I used some of the king's fifth to purchase the rest of the supplies and here is a receipt from the captain showing how much gold he is taking to Spain and how much he charged for the supplies." I opened my shirt as I concluded as if to strip myself for punishment, "I am ready to be flogged for my crime and spend time in the pillory. It is up to you."

Cortez looked at the supplies that I had purchased as well as the new men now training with the others and smiled. "I think you made a wise choice. We had to leave much of the gold in the treasure room so the king was not getting his fifth anyway. Put your shirt back on. We have work to do."

Cortez had been busy while we were gone. He had taken several small towns between Tlaxcala and the sea to form safe passage for future travel. He had also ordered ships to be built so when we attacked Tenochtitlan again we could take it from the water too. I was even more impressed when I saw that the ships had been built and then transported overland to the newly captured villages by the lake so we could go to battle again. He had also captured several small towns on the far side of the lake from Tenochtitlan.

Tenochtitlan
Cuauhtémoc Speaks

Death is around me. Cuitlahuac is dead. His successor is dead. Mexico is invaded by a second invader and that is death. I believe it is the fault of the invaders. They have sent this wasting disease on us. People are dying in the streets. Soldiers are dying in the field. My runners are dying on the way coming and going. I hear rumors that the white man has taken other cities around the lake, but I have no way of knowing. I have been elected Tlailok. I don't believe I was elected because of my great skills, but because there are so few of us left. Am I to be the last Tlailok of the Mexica?

The Mexican Valley
Esteban Speaks

A sickness is covering the Mexican valley. It hit Tlaxcala and rumors say that it is hitting Tenochtitlan. It must be across the valley. I did not hear of it in Vera Cruz so it might be a sickness from the upper elevations. Many people are dying and the army is being depleted. Since Montezuma died there have been two kings. Now the rumors say that Cuauhtémoc is the new ruler. He was one of the men who we met the first week in Mexico.

Cortez has decided to enter Tenochtitlan by way of the bridges with army and help from the boats that were built and hauled by hand to the lake. On the April 28, 1521 we started with the first attack using the boats. It was an initial success in that the boats were able to attack some canoes and send them back to the city. We attacked using the ships for the next month and on June 23 we tried an attack against one of the bridges. I was in the midst of an attack up the bridge when the Mexican soldiers started to retreat. We thought we had them so we attacked even faster up the bridge and across some shallow water. They ran further and so did we to attack and take the city. Too late we realized our error. The Mexicans came up behind us from hidden canoes and attacked us from both sides. They shoved sharpened stakes in the shallow water so if we tried to return through the shallow water we would have to force our way through the sharp stakes. I was fighting with my sword against whichever native I could attack and kill. In the distance I could see the pyramid and sacrificial stone on top. The sight of that and the memory made me fight even harder. I fell in the water and was grabbed by leg and left arm. I attacked with wide blows hoping to hit anybody. I must have succeeded because I felt the hands leave my leg. I stumbled forward between the sharpened stakes attacking the native who still held my arm with my sword. He fell away on to the sharpened stakes with a cry and I was able to escape to the bridge. The Mexicans had fallen away but I saw them carry several men with them. I said a brief prayer as I watched them being carried to the temple and certain death.

I heard a shout, "Esteban!" I looked back and from across the divide of bridge I saw Diego being carried away struggling by several natives. "Diego! No!" I shouted. But it was too late. My musket wouldn't shoot that far and we were separated by the broken bridge that had been filled with sharpened stakes. "No, no, no." I moaned. "Diego don't leave me." In the distance I could hear a shriek of pain and sudden silence followed by a shout of joy from the natives. I was lead numbly back across the bridge away from the city. Diego who had first said "hanging is too good for him" and later became my best friend was dead. I thought back to how far we had come and how close we were to the end. "It's not fair." I cried.

Cortez was angry at us for wading across the water to attack. Even though I wasn't in charge he said "You should have known better. You tried to be too big and attack too fast to make yourselves look good." He couldn't have been more angry at me than I was myself. Surely there was something I could have done to prevent Diego's death. In the end Diego was another statistic of the conquest, but he was my friend and that made it personal. I had to admit that he was right. We saw the open area and were sure we could win.

On June 30 Cortez tried again to go up another bridge. This time we got all the way in to the city before we were attacked again. Again I fought hand to hand and sword to spear. I was able to escape when Cortez called for retreat. Others were not lucky. We heard drums and saw smoke from the pyramid. We were close enough to the pyramid that the Mexicans threw heads at us. I realized with horror that the heads were those of soldiers I had fought beside the previous week. Again I looked up to see the now all too familiar sight of the naked men being thrown over the sacrificial stone and the dagger falling on the exposed chest. I threw up as I escaped down the bridge.

Tenochtitlan
Cuauhémoc Speaks

Smoking Mirror says that the next eight days are the time when Quetzalcoatl will be the weakest and his star hidden in the grave. This will be the time to attack. Now we are at the end of those eight days and Quetzalcoatl Cortez is still living. I have tried everything. I have used all the magic of Huizilopochtli and Smoking Mirror yet Cortez still comes forward. He truly does have magic stronger than our magic. He sends word that if I surrender I will be made vassal ruler. I can not do that. We must fight to the death. We shall be ruined either way so we will go down fighting.

On the last day it seemed that all was over. My family and I and our trusted friends gathered in an attempt to escape. We had a number of canoes and set off across the lake to the mainland and my house. From there maybe we could escape to some friendly city. We had made it away from the island, but one of the invaders saw us and took off in their large boat in pursuit. It was a fast boat and soon overtook us. We tried to paddle faster but he had his fire sticks pointing at us that had caused so much damage. The women were screaming and I saw that it was over. I ordered the canoes to stop and asked to be taken to the Cortez god.

I was captured and brought before Cortez. I begged him to please stab me.

Mexico City
Esteban Speaks

It is over. It took continued attacks in to the city and many Mexicans died or fled, but it is over. Cuauhtémoc tried to escape by canoe with his family and gold but we captured him. I think he might have succeeded had he gone in a regular canoe, but he used his royal canoe that had an awning and a special seat for him. I was onboard one of the boats that Cortez had ordered built while I was in Vera Cruz. We were sailing around the lake ready to fight any canoes when we saw a large number of canoes leave from the city. Thinking that it was more soldiers we started to take after them. Then I saw that one of the canoes had the awning and I called out that it might be Cuauhtémoc's canoe. We sailed as fast as we could and cried out for him to stop. They ignored us at first, but we got closer and waved our muskets at them. I saw the king wave his hand to order the canoes to stop and it was over. We took Cuauhtémoc into our ship and carried him directly to Cortez. Other ships wanted to take him, but we refused to give the king to anybody except Cortez. We landed in the city and escorted him to Cortez. By the time we got there Cuauhtémoc was in tears. He touched the dagger on Cortez' belt and said "Stab me."

Tenochtitlan was in flames. Cortez had ordered that terrible temple where so many of our men had been sacrificed to be burnt. Tenochtitlan was no longer. Mexico City was born.

Fall of the Empire

The empire was dead. Long live the empire. Cortez had taken a few hundred men and conquered a nation. Now that he was undisputed conqueror of Mexico he would make himself rich. I suppose that is the way of life. I didn't see a lot of gold come my way. I think I was able to get the gold that I had given to buy the ship's contents. I think other soldiers got enough gold to pay for a new musket or some time in port before they signed on for another voyage. I had learned a lot about myself. I might even have matured enough to make my father happy. Eventually there were complaints about Cortez and money. He was a brilliant military planner but some complained that they never got their share of the treasure. If we had been able to take everything from the treasure room at Tencohtitlan perhaps we would have been richer, but at that point there was a choice of living or carrying gold. I think some of those who carried a lot of gold ended up on the sacrificial stone with their heads mounted on a pole outside the city. I was happy that I had managed to cheat death several times. On the beach at Vera Cruz; the causeway in the last battle and when I presented myself to Cortez for using some of the King's fifth to buy gunpowder.

I decided to head back to Cuba and see what my lands looked like. Now that New Spain was part of the Spanish empire it was easy to take a ship back to Cuba. I landed in Santiago and took the chance of visiting my uncle. I knew there would be no chance of getting money from him, but I hoped he wouldn't be angry at me that he lost control of Cortez. "He set up the legal framework of the city of Vera Cruz with several of his officers and by the time he presented it to us it was a matter of Spanish law only lacking the king's signature. When I tried to protest he threw me in irons and searched my belongings to find my second book and a gold bracelet I stole. This is what happened" I said removing my shirt to show the scars on my back. "I was given a choice of the noose or becoming a foot soldier. I chose being a foot soldier." I said as I put my shirt back on. "All in all it wasn't terrible. I made it out alive and many men did not. I'll have the memories of seeing men sacrificed on the altar the rest of my life. One of my best friends was grabbed in battle just paces away from me. I saw him being carried away as he shouted my name." My uncle listened carefully and finally said, "Well he learned that legal loophole well. I used it myself in Hispanolia. I have not gained any money from the expedition and he has enriched himself. I have nothing to give you and I'll assume that he gave you nothing." I agreed that he was right. My time in New Spain had earned me little gold, but a wealth of experiences. "I suppose if I had been honest from the start I would have been given a position in the new world as some of the conquerors. As it is I am just another foot soldier home from the war. I'll visit you and my aunt and then return to the fields to see how they are." I stayed for dinner with my aunt and uncle and spent the night since it was a journey out to the fields.

The next morning I awoke early to set out for the plantation. I wondered how I would find them. It took most of the morning to make it out to the ranch and I found Juan there just as if I had never left. "Ah señor. You've come back! I never heard word that you had died so I assumed you would eventually come back." We settled down over an early lunch and rum to talk about the fields, "So I'm home now and ready to start learning again. I hope you will continue to teach me. I think I've matured a lot. Spending two days naked in a pillory and being whipped twenty lashes with a cat o nine helps a man grow up." I had removed my shirt to show Juan the scars as if I wanted to prove that I had grown up. "Yes señor, they did give you a whipping and you returned with little gold so the scars are the only thing you returned with. Was it worth it?" As I put my shirt back on I thought for a moment. Was it worth it? The scars, the memory of friends being sacrificed. The memory of that first time we saw a sacrifice that we never got used to. Fighting our way in and out of Mexico City. "Was it worth it?" I said. "I left seeking adventure and that is what I found. The adventure gave me great pain," I said, pointing at my back, "Here and here," pointing to my heart. "Yes. I'll say it was worth it. I left here as an arrogant self absorbed boy and I return as a man who is hopefully thoughtful and mature." We did little outside work the rest of the day, spending siesta time going over records and two years of mail from Spain. As I thought, my father had been concerned about the money I had borrowed for the expedition, but it had been repaid before I even left Cuba by the discreet banker so father was happy. He and mother were more concerned about my welfare as I saw in the letters they sent to Juan. Then they heard news that Cortez had proclaimed a colony of New Spain and they assumed I was still alive. "Here's the last letter I received a few weeks ago." Juan said as he pulled a final letter from his pocket. "It was addressed to me, but basically your father said that if you showed up alive I should evaluate your maturity and see if you are ready to return to Spain and report to him. If I feel that you have matured I should report that to him so he can make the evaluation of whether to call you back to Spain." I started to say something and he continued, "Señor I don't want to be the man who determines your future. You send a letter to your father and tell him everything you told me. I'm sure he will call you back." I smiled at his trust. "Juan, I'm going to set your mind at ease. Yes. I'll write to my father and no I'm not going back yet. I might have learned a lot while I was gone, but taking care of plantations wasn't one of them. You still have some work to do."

And so we set to work. I learned everything I could about planting and management. I continued learning about bookkeeping, but this time with only one book. I learned about the slaves we had imported to work the fields. "We could not do this work without the slaves," commented Juan. I paused in my work. True. We could not do this work without the slaves. I thought to the women I had coupled with. That's what they were. Slaves. Sex slaves given by parents or tribe to the conquerors. It was all a part of war and had been back to the first war whenever that was. I thought about the woman Cortez gave me, "Use her well," was his beer filled command. And I had. I had taken her right to the brush and raped her there. That's what it was. I had raped the girl within earshot of her parents and the crew. I put down my pen, "I'll be back. I'm going to take a walk." I wonder what her name was? I thought as I walked through the fields. I guess it wouldn't make a difference if I knew her name. I wondered about the other women: some paid, but most not. Some fought and when I was done lay there while I hitched up my trousers and left. Other women just lay there with resignation at their fate. Too few had seemed to actually enjoy the act. I wondered again how many children I had sired in New Spain. I supposed these children would be part of a new race in New Spain. Malinche had already had a child by Cortez named Martin. Giving up my thoughts for the time being I returned to work. I couldn't change practices that had been in place since time began, nor was I willing to be celibate. Even the priests, with the exception of Aguilar couldn't do that.

I redoubled my efforts at work, and stayed away from the brothels in Santiago for several months. I felt happy keeping the plantation running and learning things, but something was missing. At first I thought abstinence had made me introspective, but realized it was something different. I was missing the excitement and adventure of war. Was I really that much like Cortez that I couldn't settle down to doing a normal job. I was stuck in my quandary. I couldn't decide if I missed the war and yet I felt guilty about things I had done during the conquest.

Finally my needs won out over my guilt and I announced to Juan that I would be gone for a couple nights to Santiago. As if reading my mind he said, "Si Señor. Have fun and I hope you are well rested when you return." I grunted in acknowledgment. The brothel I chose had a bar attached with inflated beer prices, but the selection of girls was usually pretty good. I sat there drinking a beer biding my time till I asked for the other selection. I heard the door open and a loud 'Esteban!" I looked up and to my amazement was Cortez. He gave me a hearty clap on the back and bought me another beer. "So you're back on your fields?" he questioned. "Yes. I'm staying here till I learn enough about management and someday my father will call me back to Spain. In the meantime I'm learning and keeping the plantation running." If he bore any ill will for my theft on the expedition he didn't show it. But that's the way he is: always magnanimous in victory. Quick to jump on faults or perceived faults, but generous in victory. "But you. What are you doing here? I thought you would be back in Spain or staying in New Spain." He paused for a moment. "Yes. Well I came back to take care of business here. My wife left Cuba and went to New Spain. She didn't last too long there and she died. I'm here settling the affairs I have here and then I'll be back to New Spain and later Spain." I knew that his wife had gone to Mexico and Cortez had been surprised at her arrival. She had died under mysterious circumstances a few weeks later. That news had circled back to Cuba, but I wasn't going to admit to knowing it or asking questions. I had scars on my back for crossing Cortez. Instead I said, "I'm sorry about the death of your wife. I hope you get her business taken care of so you can return to New Spain." He moved in his chair. "Well there's another reason I'm here too. I kind of hoped I would find you still in Cuba. I want to propose another expedition and I want you to come with me. But look. Here comes the madam. It's time to choose our girls. We will have fun tonight and talk business tomorrow. My treat!"

If he was expecting me to have a good time that night after announcing he wanted me to go on another expedition he was certainly mistaken. I chose a girl and took her off to one of the little curtained off rooms that gave a semblance of privacy, but little else. I could hear Cortez laughing and other sounds of the business of pleasure. Between the beer and his words I had my mind on anything but sex. I didn't perform well and the girl finally took my money and left in search of another man or an evening without work.

The next morning Cortez and I sat down for the bread and weak tea that amounted to breakfast here, "So did you think about what I said?" asked Cortez. "Think about it? I couldn't do anything else last night thinking about it. Where do you want to go and why do you want me?" I asked. "Well, to tell you the truth I always was sorry that I had to make an example of you in Vera Cruz. You deserved it though. Remember that. But you turned yourself around and became a valuable fighter as well as a good businessman when you bought the supplies for our final battle. I need that on my next expedition." I looked at him, "Well I'll admit that I deserved the flogging and more and I'll say that it helped me become a better man. If I ever forget all I have to do is feel the scars on my back and ass. But where do you want to go next? Isn't one country enough?" Cortez looked at me. "I want to go to Guatemala and put down the insurrection there. I'm yearning for adventure again and government administration is not going to do it for me. Come with me. We will have another adventure before you settle down in Spain."

I convinced Cortez to come out to the plantation with me so we could talk. It was true that I was somewhat like Cortez in that I wanted an adventure, but also I didn't look forward to more battles or the fear of sacrifice again. "I don't think you need to fear that anymore. I want to go overland though Guatemala to get to my area past there. The governor I installed has gone against me and I aim to put him out and take back my land. I had forgotten that Cortez had taken territory to the SouthWest of Cuba on the mainland. He must have discovered or thought that he could go overland from Mexico to arrive there. In my mind nobody had done that before. "It shall be a wonderful trip. I'm taking entertainers and chefs so we can travel in style. Malinche will be going as translator. She speaks Spanish now so we don't have to worry. I'm also bringing Cuauhtémoc as I can't trust him to not revolt against me."

I took this opportunity to ask him something that had been bothering me, "Remember all the women we picked up? Did it ever bother you that we only used them for sex?" Cortez looked at me like I was crazy. "Only for sex? Don't you remember that they cleaned and cooked for us too? Are you getting a soft heart? This is war and women are one of the spoils of war. They're better off now than they were before, don't forget it!"

"Yes I know. I was just thinking about that woman you gave me in Vera Cruz and I took her to the brush and fucked her right there. You probably heard me from the town." Cortez laughed, "Of course we heard you. We laughed all the way through." I told him about the time Mateo and Santiago and I took turns fucking her and I didn't even know her name. "Well. She probably didn't know your name either. Listen. That's war. Santiago didn't want to be sacrificed on the altar, but he was. He knew the dangers going to war. Women get taken every day. That's one of the results of war. We brought peace and stability to Mexico. She doesn't have to worry about her children being given up or captured for sacrifice. She is better now for our coming even if she did have to have your child, and couple with your tiny cock" He concluded with a hearty slap on my back. "Come on now man. Are you coming with me or not?"

I had to admit it sounded like an adventure, and much safer than conquering a nation. I told Cortez that I would think about it, and I would be in touch with him later. Cortez, sensing the brushoff, smiled and said "OK you think about it, but maybe your heart lies elsewhere. Now I think I'll ask Juan to find me a ride or driver to take me back to Santiago."

I watched him leave, and thought about his last statement. Maybe my heart did lie elsewhere. If it was gold I sought, I would not find it in another adventure, just as I had not found it in Mexico. Maybe there was more to life than adventure, conquering the New World, or putting down an insurrection. Maybe I could find adventure in Spain. Maybe I could learn to be a man there too. True, Cortez had offered me a leading role in this voyage, but could I be sure I would not cross him again. In reality Cortez wanted titles and gold and would stop at nothing to get them. Anybody in his way short of the king, he would try to push aside. No, I thought, my heart does lie elsewhere, and that is back in Spain. In Spain I would have to submit to my father again, but that would be a lot easier now than when I was sixteen. I think I am mature enough now that I would not be an embarrassment to my father.

August 13, 1522
Santiago, Cuba

Dear Father, it is now one year to the day since the fall of the Mexican empire and I want to tell you about my time in Mexico. It was hard, I escaped death several times, but came out wiser. The first time was when I signed on with Cortez and he appointed me as accountant. I was so intent on making money I kept two books. The first book I showed Cortez and the second one was only for myself. I was trying to make money off of the expedition by stealing from king and crew. Cortez found the book and sentenced me to two dozen lashes, and he also reduced me in position to soldier. Rather, he gave me the choice of the noose or being a soldier. I chose being a soldier. It took several days to recover from my wounds and I lost all my friends. The other soldiers regarded me as a thief, which is what I was. Father Aguilar acted as the mediator between myself and some of the soldiers and I made some friends. I'm sure you heard the story that we had several battles before we reached Mexico City. The truth of our situation I saw the first morning when we saw a group of men being being dragged to the temple to be sacrificed there. You've heard stories about the sacrifices, so we lived in fear for the next couple of years that we would be caught and sacrificed to their pagan god. I avoided death again when Cortez sent me back to Veracruz to get supplies and I used some of the gold that was part of the King's Fifth to buy supplies from a passing ship. I could have been killed for that but Cortez thought it was a good idea. Once the final battle was over I made it back to Cuba with no gold and no gold for my uncle. I went back to the to the plantation and continued to learn with Juan, and I have learned a lot about bookkeeping and running a plantation. I have matured a lot over the last couple of years and I have the scars to show it and I believe that I am mature enough now to come back and work for you. I'm sorry for the pain I must have caused you when I was younger. I promise that I will not do that again. I have gained a new respect for women and will show more restraint in the future. I will abide by any decision you make.

Your loving son,

Esteban.

What's True and What's False

Obviously Cortez was a real person. He was quick to perceive a fault and magnanimous in victory. Sources indicate that on the beach at Veracruz a group of men rebelled and Cortez ordered that one of them have his foot chopped off. I just changed that to Esteban and the pillory. Cortez's wife did die under mysterious circumstances. Cortez did go to Guatemala and killed Cuauhtemoc during the journey.

Esteban is a fictional character, but Velasquez was the governor of Cuba. Velasquez did try to manage Cortez but found that impossible. He failed in stopping the voyage and later in his efforts to arrest Cortez. I don't know if Velasquez had a nephew much less if he came to Cuba, but that's the joy of writing fiction.

Father Aguilar was real. He really did ask "Is today Wednesday?" He seems to have disappeared after the conquest so I do not know what happened to him. Guerrero did choose to stay behind because he had found a wife.

Malinche seems to have left a mixed legacy. Sometimes she is called a traitor to her race. Others say that she made the best of a bad situation. I went with the later. She did have a son by Cortez and he eventually returned to Spain. Sources indicate that she lived out her life in Mexico City.

I finished this book in November of 2016 and I continued editing through January 2017. In March I was diagnosed with ALS and spent seven weeks in the hospital. I am now on ventilator and tube feeding with no use of arms or hands. My thanks to my nurse Dan who very patiently scrolled through the document for me and made the changes I dictated. Big thanks to my brother and sister-in-law for letting me stay with them and taking care of me.

Made in the USA
Las Vegas, NV
06 August 2024